THE JOURNAL of ANGELA ASHBY

Other books by Liana Gardner

7th Grade Revolution

Awards

7th Grade Revolution

Winner in Pre-Teen Fiction (Ages 10-12)
2018 American Fiction Awards
Finalist in Children's Fiction
2018 International Book Awards
Honorable Mention in Children's Fiction
2018 Hollywood Book Festival

The Journal of Angela Ashby

Honorable Mention in Children's Fiction
2018 Hollywood Book Festival

The Journal of Angela Ashby

Liana Gardner

▼

The Journal of Angela Ashby

Cover and Interior Illustrations by Sam Shearon
www.mister-sam.com

ISBN: 978-1-944109-69-1

VESUVIAN BOOKS

Published by Vesuvian Books
www.vesuvianbooks.com

Printed in the United States of America

10 9 8 7 6 5 4 3 2 1

Table of Contents

For Sammie

"With great power comes great responsibility."

~ Voltaire

Chapter One - The Carnival

I have great power.

That's what she told me. The old fortune-teller at the school carnival.

I thought I had done the right thing ... with the magic journal she gave me. But nothing could prepare me for what happened next.

Or, for what I unleashed.

My cutoffs inched their way up and tried to give me a wedgie. I tugged at the hem in an attempt to make them longer before I knocked on the door. I'd grown so much, none of my clothes fit.

Mrs. Chan opened the door and smiled. "Come on in, Angela. Mallory isn't ready yet."

I strode through the door. "Is she in her room? Can I go back?" Not waiting for her answer, I hurried to Mallory's room and knocked before throwing the door open.

Everything in the room was princess pink, from the wall color to the bedspread and pillow shams, to the carpet underfoot. Boy band and movie posters covered every available inch.

Mallory sat on the stool in front of her vanity, brushing her hair, but still wore her pajamas.

She shook her brush at me. "One day you're going to burst in on me, and I'm not going to be decent."

I snorted. "Like you're ever ready on time. And if it happens, I'll gouge my eyes out."

She eyed my shorts and opened her mouth.

I held up my hand. "One word about my shorts, and we can talk about the four-year-old pink of your room."

Her mouth snapped shut and she frowned. "I'm going to redecorate."

Yeah, like she hadn't said *that* fifty times before.

She gathered her hair into a ponytail to brush the ends free of tangles.

I plopped on her bed. "Mom hasn't had time to take me shopping and Dad hasn't given her the money yet." Mom and I always had so much fun shopping for new clothes before school started. Except this year. Because of the divorce.

Mallory opened her closet and searched through the rack.

A spurt of irritation flared as she struggled to pull them apart. She had so many clothes she'd outgrow them before she wore them even once. Too bad I wasn't the same size ... I could borrow half her wardrobe and she'd never notice.

"Oh." She faced me and put one hand on her hip. "We have to take Kirky with us because Dad can't watch him today." She sighed and went back to the task at hand.

I kicked my feet back and forth. "No problem. I like your little brother. He's so cute."

"Having a younger brother is not all fun and games." She glanced at me over her shoulder and raised an eyebrow. "He can be a pain sometimes."

Mallory didn't know how lucky she was. She at least had a *whole* family, while mine had been torn apart. I'd always wanted a baby brother or sister—but that was never gonna happen now. Dad had left Mom and me and married Holly-the-homewrecker.

I fell back on the bed and stared at the ceiling. "Hurry up, already. By the time you're dressed, the carnival will be over."

I searched for pictures in the lumpy surface, like indoor cloud gazing. A dragon with wings unfurled stood next to a

~ 3 ~

howling wolf.

"Why are you always in such a hurry?"

I stopped looking for images in the cottage-cheese ceiling bumps and thought for a moment. "I guess because I don't want to miss out on anything."

"I'll be back in a couple minutes. Try not to explode with impatience because I don't want to have to clean up the mess."

"Ha-ha."

The smell of popping kettle corn melded with cotton candy and funnel cakes filled the air. The sweet scent almost overwhelmed me. Booths and tents ranged in rows across the athletic field and rides were in the center of the track; a Ferris wheel, a megaslide, a rock climbing wall, and a Tasmanian Twister. Bells, whistles, excited squeals, the cries of booth vendors hawking their games, mingled with conversations.

"Come on." Mallory tugged on my arm. "I wanna see what they have."

Now she was in a hurry.

Mrs. Chan put a hand on Mallory's shoulder while the other kept a tight grip on Kirky's wrist.

He'd already escaped twice since we'd arrived because Mallory's mom couldn't find his leash before we left. Until Kirky learned to walk, I had thought leashes were for dogs. But the boy was an escape artist, and tying something to him was the only way to keep track of him.

"Let's check in with each other in two hours. Meet me by the dunk tank over by the sand. Have fun." The last words were said to our backs.

Mallory and I made a beeline for the booths. I wanted to play as many games as we had time for. We wove our way through the people clogging the aisles. Mallory stopped by a booth sporting hats with bling, but I kept moving. If I didn't, we'd be stuck there all day while Mallory looked at each one. I snorted. As if she needed another hat.

I didn't see Cynthia until she blocked my way.

"Nice shorts, Ash-can. Did you borrow them from your doll?"

Did she have to be so vile? "You're just jealous they won't fit you."

Mallory walked up behind Cynthia. I bit back a laugh. The two were so mismatched. Mallory, short, slender, with long, dark hair and the perfect porcelain skin of her ancestors, wore square-framed glasses, which slid down her nose. She stopped short and her knees trembled.

In front of Mallory stood Gargantua. As much as she tried, Mallory never could quite hide her fear of Cynthia. I kept trying to tell her it only made the bullying worse.

"Of course they won't fit me. I'm a beautiful Amazon."

"If you mean you're from the Amazon Rainforest, your skin is the wrong color and you're too tall to come from one of the pygmy tribes." I sneered. "They prefer bronzed goddesses to a baboon-faced troll with a red mop on her head."

Her fingers curled and face scrunched.

"Awww, if you meant an Amazon like Wonder Woman, well ..." I drew the word out. Did I really want to push her hard so early in the day?

"Wonder Woman has nothing on me." Cynthia tossed her red curls over her shoulder and spied Mallory. "Well, if it isn't MAL-feasance."

Mallory's eyes widened and she took a small step back.

My face got hot. I couldn't stand the way Cynthia picked on Mallory. "Oh, good for you, SINnnn-thia. You learned a vocabulary word. Can you use it properly in a sentence?"

Mallory hid a grin behind her hand.

Cynthia's red face clashed with her hair, a horrible sight. She moved closer until our noses almost touched. "You looking for trouble, Ash-can?"

"That's so old, Benson. Why don't you come up with something fresh?" Patting my mouth, I gave an exaggerated yawn. "At least you're picking on someone closer to your own size."

Before Cynthia could respond, Mallory grabbed my arm. "Ang ... Angela, c-c-c-come on. We gotta go. My m-m-mom will be w-w-waiting."

What? We just left Mrs. Chan and didn't have to meet her for two hours.

"P-p-p-oor, M-m-m-m-allory." Cynthia sprayed spit as she jeered. "C-c-c-an't even get the w-w-w-w-ords out."

I clenched my jaw. I couldn't stand Cynthia mocking Mallory's stutter. She only had it when she got nervous. I raised a fist, but Mallory gave a slight shake of her head.

Oh. Enlightenment dawned. She had made up an excuse to get away from Cynthia.

"Aw, sorry we can't stay and chat, Cyndy. Toodles." I waggled my fingers at her and let Mallory pull me away before Cynthia erupted. Although I was sure I'd get extra points if I made her head blow up.

"Angela, you know you shouldn't play with the trolls." Mallory pushed her black-framed glasses back into place. "Do you have to bait her?"

"Yes. Especially when she makes fun of you." I put my hand on her shoulder. "You don't think I'm gonna stand by and let her pick on my best friend in the whole wide world, do you?"

"She is so mean." Mallory's brows furrowed. She slowed next to a rack of purses. "When do you think your mom will be able to take you shopping?"

"I don't know. Lately, she always has to work extra. She told me I should ask my dad to take me when I see him tomorrow." I looked over my shoulder to make sure Cynthia wasn't following us.

She stood glowering where we'd left her.

We stopped at the baseball throw booth. I bought a chance and took the three balls. I aimed then threw the ball as hard as I could. Missed. "Can you imagine how embarrassing? How would you like to have your dad take you clothes shopping?"

"No way." Her nose wrinkled in disgust. "Have you seen my dad's clothes? I'd be mortified. My life would be Ooooover."

Mallory, the drama queen.

I took aim with ball number two and hucked it at the bottles. Shoot. I nicked one, but the bottle didn't fall. "But I need new clothes, and Mom doesn't have the time." And money was tight if Dad didn't help out. Having divorced parents sucked.

The sun glinted off Mallory's glasses and masked her expression. "Why don't we see if my mom can take you instead?"

"Really? You think she would?" I tossed the ball in the air then caught it.

"Sure. I finally talked the parentals into redecorating my bedroom so it doesn't look like an overgrown toddler lives there."

"About time." I tossed the ball up again to keep from rolling my eyes over Mallory referring to her parents as *the parentals*.

"We're going to the mall today anyway, so why not throw in a little clothes shopping, too?" She tilted her head. "I could use a new purse …"

"How're you going to redo your room?" I had to stop her thinking about clothes shopping before she dragged me through sixteen stores, all of which didn't have the kind of clothes I liked best. Comfortable.

A raspy voice interrupted us. "Are you gonna take your last

throw?"

I glanced over my shoulder.

The man running the booth leaned forward, an unlit stogie clenched in his teeth. "You're holdin' up the line."

"Mister, are you supposed to have a filthy cigar on school grounds?"

His chin shook as he frowned. I'd better throw the ball before he came over the counter after it. I turned and fired.

Direct hit. Bottom center.

With a satisfying crash, the entire pyramid wobbled and fell.

Mallory and I took a few steps away.

"Hey, kid." His voiced scratched out. "Don'cha wan'chur prize?" He held out two sport soaker balls—a baseball and a football.

I grabbed them and handed the football to Mallory. "Stellar prize, right?"

"Well, if we had about fifty, and a good hiding place, and ambushed someone, we'd have a blast. But with two? Not so much."

I tapped her arm. "So? What about your room?"

Mallory moved out of the aisle and stood in the shade at the side of a booth.

"I want to do a black and white scheme."

I smirked. "You're going from a room where the Disney princesses puked pink everywhere to zebra land?"

"Hey." Her nose wrinkled and her lips scrunched. "I

remember your room ..."

"All right, I get it." We were both embarrassed by our childhood decorating taste. "Sorry. So tell me what else, besides black and white?"

She leaned against the booth. "I saw the coolest wall mural on the internet. It's a picture of an enormous spiral staircase with a black wrought iron banister and white steps taken from the top looking down." Her eyes gleamed. "It's like looking into a tunnel that goes on forever."

I grinned. "It does sound cool."

Her eyes grew wistful. "Now all I need is to convince my mom to buy it for me."

I brushed my shoulder against hers. "You will. Your folks agreed to redo your room, and they'll want you to be happy with it." I took a step back. "Come on, let's go see what else there is."

As we checked out the rest of the booths, the sun got hotter. We made our way to the outside edge of the aisles, where the crowd thinned and the noise level dropped. The line for the Hi-Striker looked short. I veered in that direction.

Zachary Taylor grabbed the mallet and stepped up to the launch pad.

Whacking something with a hammer—what a good idea. "I want to do this and then we can finish looking at the rest of the stuff."

Zach rested the hammer head against the ground and wiped his sweaty palms off on his tan cargo shorts before grabbing a handful of chalk. A fine mist of chalk dust covered his legs and turned his dark skin, gray. He hefted the mallet up to his shoulder and he took a step to steady himself from the weight. The mallet was almost as big as he was.

I rested my hand on my hip. "Does that sound like a plan?"

Mallory couldn't take her eyes off him as the hammer head quivered.

What did she see in Zach? His curly black hair looked like it had been styled by a tornado, except the three curls he carefully placed on his forehead. With a slight frame, knobby knees and elbows, and thick-framed glasses, he wasn't exactly heartthrob material. At least with Mallory, it didn't matter that he was short.

I nudged her shoulder. "Mallory?"

She kept her eyes on Zach. "Sure. Sounds fine."

He swung the mallet and missed the strike pad. It thudded against the ground and he dropped it and shook his hands. Must've hurt.

But he regripped the mallet and took another swing. Success. This time the disk rose three-quarters of the way to the bell before falling back down to the bottom.

I prodded Mallory's shoulder. "Do you want to give it a try?"

She took a deep breath. "Sure."

The way she held the mallet, we were in for disaster. Instead of gripping it with both hands together, one was up by the head and the other at the end of the shaft. She'd never get enough velocity to send the disk up the pole. I bit my tongue to keep from laughing. She couldn't even raise the mallet in the air. At least she didn't miss the strike pad. But the disk, as predicted, moved a few inches and no more.

"Oh, Fairy Farts!" Mallory leaned the mallet against the striker.

I snickered. She always said *fairy farts* when irritated.

My turn. I paid for my chance, grabbed the mallet and thought of all the things going wrong with my life. Clothes that didn't fit were the tip of the divorce garbage heap.

I whirled the mallet through the air. Direct hit.

The disk whizzed up the pole. *Ding.* Then fell back to earth.

Add another useless prize to the collection for the day.

"Nice one, Angela." Zach tried to look nonchalant as he leaned up against a post, his legs crossed casually and his left foot firmly planted in dog poop.

"Thanks. And, uh, Zach? You might want to clean off your shoes."

He looked at the ground and his face turned a dusky red. "Let's go, Mal."

She waved. "See you around, Zach."

He wiped his shoe on the trodden grass. "Later, Mallory."

I giggled as we walked off. "Why is he always an accident waiting to happen?"

"Be nice." Mallory flicked my arm. "Think how you'd feel in his shoes?"

"Stinky." I rolled with laughter. I couldn't help it.

Mallory's brows lowered as she frowned.

I jabbed her in the side. "You like Zach?"

She crossed her arms. "No."

Yeah, right.

We reached the farthest row where a tent stood at the end. Worn, patched curtains covered the opening. It looked like a strong wind could blow it to the ground. The tent didn't belong. The rest of the booths were in good repair, sturdy, and looked new.

"Let's go find something to drink." I wiped sweat off my brow.

"Or we need to find some shade." Mallory turned to go back, then stopped.

Where did all the people come from? A rippling mass filled the aisle. The last thing I wanted to do was make my way back through the throng.

Mallory crossed her arms. "If we go down the aisle we'll get body slammed. Or ..." She drew the word out. "We could check out what's in that tent."

I glanced at the tent again. It should be in another place and time. Like in a ghost town. "I don't know, Mal. It looks odd."

Mallory narrowed her eyes. "Not odd, a fortune-teller tent. It'd be kinda fun to have our fortunes told."

"How do you know ...?" My words trailed off and I blinked. A sign had appeared on the side of the tent. The oval sign had an eye in the center and the words Madame Vadoma above in gold letters, with 'Fortunes Told' below. Why hadn't I seen the sign before?

I grabbed her arm. "What happens if we go inside and the fortune-teller is a psycho mass murderer who kills us and keeps our eyes in a jar as trophies?"

She hesitated then pushed my shoulder. "Ew. That's gross. How do you come up with things like that anyway?" She held up her hand. "No. Don't tell me. I don't want to know."

I laughed. I couldn't help teasing her, she was so squeamish. "You really want to go have some fraud tell you a bunch of stuff that's never going to happen?"

Mallory put her hand on her right hip. "How do you know she's a fraud?"

I rolled my eyes. "Come on, Mal. A fortune-teller at the school carnival? How good's she gonna be?" But we still had over an hour before we had to meet her mom. And it would be cooler inside. I shrugged. "Okay. Let's go have our fortunes told."

Chapter Two - The Fortune

We pulled back the cloth door and stepped inside. After the bright sunlight, the gloom inside the tent spread into every crevice. Once the curtain closed, the popcorn and funnel cake aroma disappeared and the outside noise fell silent. Neither hot or cold, we had entered a vacuum.

The tent had two rooms. We stood in the entry room, unsure whether to call out. The combination of darkness and silence made prickles run up my spine.

"Welcome." The voice, deep and penetrating, cut through the darkness from the other room.

I started and Mallory clutched my arm. It sounded like the voice of the Bulgarian butcher at the market—the one who had the slightly crazed look in his eye when swinging his cleaver.

"I be with you soon."

A black cloth blocked my view and I shivered.

Mallory sucked in her cheeks as she stared at the cloth. "M-m-maybe this wasn't such a good i-i-idea."

Her whisper barely reached my ears.

I removed my arm from her vise-like grip and rubbed the white marks her fingers left to get the circulation going again. "We'll be fine. The dark makes it seem spooky."

More than the dark made it spooky, but Mallory was already keyed up enough. Although reluctant at first, I wanted to see what would happen. My eyes adjusted to the dark interior, helped by the ray of light coming through a hole in the top of the tent.

The black curtain moved and something small and low to the ground streaked out. Mallory yelped.

I followed its progress until it stopped near the tent siding, just out of the ray of light.

"It's okay, Mal." I nudged her arm. "Look, it's just a black cat."

The cat sat and stared at us through amber-colored eyes, unmoving except a rhythmic twitch of the end of its tail.

I regretted my earlier teasing because Mallory trembled. Sometimes being scared was fun, like in a haunted house, because nothing bad would really happen. But this felt different.

Electricity filled the air and the hairs on my arms stood up. In the quiet, each tick of Mallory's watch twanged my nerves. Waiting caused my feet to itch, like they wanted to run.

Mallory's cheeks lost the pink tint from being in the sun, although flushed cheeks were preferable to the pallor taking their place.

"Why do I feel like we're in the middle of a Scooby-Doo episode?" She giggled, but her nervousness came through.

"Well, if we're in an episode of Scooby-Doo, then you're Velma because you're short, dark-haired and wear glasses, so that makes me the beautiful Daphne." I pretended to fluff my hair.

The cat raised a paw and licked it. Was it mimicking me?

"A Chinese Velma?" Mallory squeaked as she tried to suppress a laugh. "If I'm Velma, then I'm the intelligent one. And when you walk through the curtain, you'll get kidnapped."

"If I get kidnapped, you'd better roundup someone to stand in for Freddie and Shaggy and come rescue me." I stuck my tongue out at her.

A ring encrusted hand thrust the curtain back and we both jumped.

Lighthearted moment over.

A tall, thin woman followed the hand into the room. Her big eyes were circled with thick, black liner that trailed up at the corners. And dark-red lipstick made her mouth look like a bloody gash. Her prominent nose and angular cheeks gave her a hawk-like appearance.

"I am Madame Vadoma."

Dressed all in black, she wore several thick, braided silver chains. The longest chain held a pendant—a large multi-colored oval stone at the top with a smaller round stone underneath and a teardrop stone pointing to the ground. On all ten fingers she wore rings, the largest looked like a jumble of jewels; green, red, blue, yellow, rounded, squared, tear-drop, both large and small. Her hoop earrings swayed and full skirt swished, rustling against her boots as she stalked toward us.

She had certainly dressed the part of a fortune-teller. The only thing missing was a vibrant scarf tied on her head with the long tails trailing down her back.

When she stopped under the ray of light from the hole in the tent, I noticed her amber-colored eyes—the same color as the cat's. I glanced at where the cat had been, but it was gone.

"You." She pointed her index finger at Mallory, and the fiery opal she wore winked in the light. "Come with me."

Mallory froze and I thought she might crumple, so I put my mouth next to her ear. "Remember, you're Velma. You'll be fine."

The woman held the curtain back. "No need to be afraid. I will give you good fortune."

When the curtain fell back into place, silence descended again.

Decorations I hadn't noticed before popped out of the shadows as I swept my gaze around the tent. A standing Buddha statue guarded the entrance. How had I missed him when we came in? The happy statue had a pot-belly and a bare chest with chains around his neck. Geesh, his earlobes were big. I approached the table to the side of the Buddha.

A large lavender orb sat on a polished wooden base. I smirked. I should've expected to find a crystal ball in a fortune-teller's tent. No fortune-teller would be complete without it. But the cloudiness of the orb surprised me because I expected the crystal ball to be clear. How would you see the fortune in something cloudy?

As I gazed, shapes shifted in the orb. *Whoa.* I blinked and took a couple steps back. That was kinda freaky.

It must have been a trick of the poor lighting.

Moving closer, I peered deeply into the crystal. If I closed my eyes, I'd be able to see Madame Vadoma rubbing the ball and muttering incantations. I snickered. Madame Vadoma was probably a stage name. I imagined her at home, where everyone knew her as Maggie Scruggs or something like it, sitting in a frumpy bathrobe sipping tea and eating popcorn while watching the news on TV.

Madame Vadoma, *puh-leeeze.* Such an obvious fraud. But she had Mallory conned.

To the side of the crystal ball sat a green skull about the size of a large grapefruit. I picked it up to get a better look. The rock was kinda cool—green, with turquoise colored dots and lines swirling through it. The stone had been polished, so it was smooth to the touch, except for a few crevices on the top. I set it next to the orb again.

The next object on the table was a Zen garden, complete with a miniature tree called a bonsai. Right after the divorce Mom tried growing a bonsai. She said it was supposed to help bring serenity when clipping it. It didn't last a week before I saw the remains in the trash, a stubby stick, with no leaves. Since Dad left, neither of us had serenity and it was all Holly's fault for stealing him away from us.

I stared at the swirls in the Zen garden sand. The marks

outlined the rocks and tree, and between rocks wavy lines flowed like a sand river. In the open area a large swirl, like a sea snail's shell—tightly wound in the center, growing larger with each loop—met the swirls outlining the stones.

A rake lay next to the garden. Without thinking, I picked it up and raked through the sand. A sense of peace came over me as I made swirly marks. Maybe a Zen garden was what Mom needed.

When the curtain opened my heart raced. I dropped the rake and spun around.

Mallory beamed and she clutched a small cloth bag in her hands. "Angela, you have to go with Madame Vadoma. It was so much fun."

Madame Vadoma held the curtain open. "Come with me."

As I passed Mallory, I winked. "Just remember to get Freddie and Shaggy to help rescue me." I swept past Madame Vadoma and into the next room.

Two chairs stood on opposite sides next to a table. An arc of cards, face down, lay in the middle between two lit candles. The cards had a decorative back. A Ferris wheel loomed over a carnival tent while the fog rolled in. A little worse for wear, the tent looked eerily like the one we were in. Coincidence?

She strode to the far side of the table. "Sit."

I sat in the indicated chair and suppressed a giggle. I wondered whether I would soon be meeting a tall, handsome stranger, or taking a long vacation to exotic places.

Madame Vadoma ran the back of her hand over the cards.

"Please. Take ten cards and hand them to me."

I selected one from the center of the deck. When I flipped it over, it was a regular playing card. The kind Mallory and I used to play *War* and *Go Fish* with. How could Madame Vadoma tell my fortune with plain playing cards? Maybe she played solitaire while waiting to tell someone's fortune.

The candles hissed and sputtered sending coils of smoke upward. As soon as I handed the card to Madame Vadoma, the wick burned steadily with barely a wisp of smoke. *Spooky.*

Wanting to get this fortune over, I quickly picked cards from either end, and slowly worked my way back to the center. After handing over the requested ten cards, I sat back and stifled a smirk.

Madame Vadoma held them, closed her eyes, and took a deep breath. When she exhaled, she opened her eyes and rapidly laid the cards out in front of her. The candle flames grew as she put the cards on the table.

The way she put the cards on the table was different than any game of solitaire I'd ever seen. Some were placed across the table, and others were in a column. One of the cards, the three of spades gave me an uneasy feeling, while the ten of hearts felt happy. Weird. I'd never thought about feelings with cards before.

She held her palm over the cards, then looked straight into my eyes. "You have much upheaval in your life and you feel lonely."

My breath was sucked out of me. This no longer felt like

some parlor trick. How did she know about my parents' divorce and my being alone so much? The intensity of her stare felt like she was able to see straight through me and into my thoughts. Uncomfortable, I glanced down at the cards.

In the middle of the layout the Ace of Spades drew me in. Smoke from the candles created a foggy layer and the image wavered and morphed into a winged hooded figure carrying a scythe through a graveyard. *The angel of death.* I blinked and ran a hand over my eyes. Once I lowered my hand, the card showed the black spade and letter 'A'. Nothing else. Not even a gravestone.

I didn't imagine it. Or maybe it would be better if I had. I gazed back at Madame Vadoma.

"You will gain power beyond your wildest imaginings and need to use it wisely."

Yeah, right. What twelve-year-old ever had power? We were back to the usual phony reading. I settled back into my chair to wait for the line about the dark stranger.

Madame Vadoma narrowed her eyes. "Young lady, this is not trick done for amusement. I give you caution. You would be wise to pay heed."

Was she reading my mind?

"You have struggles ahead as you learn to use your power. Temptation will beckon and you will want to use it for ill. You must resist. Down the path of ill-will lies destruction."

Weren't these things supposed to be light, fluffy readings about finding love and fortune? Ill-will and destruction were not supposed to be part of the deal.

Her amber eyes bore into mine. "You have choices to make about the power of your heart. Casual choice makes trouble. Be cautious with desires. The right choices will lead you to happiness and fulfillment."

A shiver ran through my body and goose pimples dotted my arms. The words sounded like the usual trickery. Besides, I could hear the same lecture from my mom. Make the wrong choices and you get in trouble. Make the right choices and you'll be happy. *Big deal.*

So why were the hairs standing on my arms?

Madame Vadoma grabbed a thin leather book lying on the table beside her. She ran her hands over the cover and mumbled words I didn't understand. Her claw-like hands grasped the book as she stared at me. Her gaze penetrated my soul and as much as I wanted to, I couldn't look away.

Her eyes widened at something behind me. With one hand she clutched the book closer to her body, then blew twice in rapid succession on the fingertips of her other hand. Tingles ran down my spine and I snapped my head around to look over my shoulder. Nothing was there. *Creepy.*

She closed her eyes and the tensions drained from her arms and shoulders. Taking a deep breath, her lids fluttered open and she met my gaze. Madame Vadoma grunted and gave a nod, which sent her hoops swinging. "I give you this. It is for you to write what is in your heart." She handed me the book. "Remember your heart has power. Use it wisely." She stood.

"Keep your heart pure, and you will do no harm."

Things were getting a little too freaky. Hugging the book to my chest, I shot out of my seat. "Um, thanks for the reading."

Backing up a few steps, I turned and bolted through the curtain.

Chapter Three - Madame Vadoma Disappears

Mallory took one look at my face, and her jaw dropped. "What's the matter?"

"Nothing." I kept moving toward the outer door. "We have to get back to your mom. Are we late?"

Mallory checked her watch. "We still have time."

I grabbed her arm and pulled. "Come on, Mal. Let's go."

Once we stepped out into the bright sunshine, my heart slowed and my panic diminished. The heat of the day hit like molten lava and the smell of frying grease and overcooked hotdogs floated in the air. I felt like someone had flipped a switch—I heard the squeals, bells, clanging and murmurs of the crowd again. I released my grip on Mallory's arm.

"What got into you? Did you see a ghost or something?"

"I don't know."

"What do you mean?" Mallory's eyes widened. "You saw a ghost?"

"No. Madame Vadoma creeped me out." I headed toward the crowded aisles. "At the end, she got all freaky, looking around the room like she was scared and blowing on her fingers." I didn't know whether to tell her about the card changing … she might think I'd gone crazy.

"Really?" Mallory's voice trailed up. "She calmed me down and told me the nicest things. She even gave me a crystal." She opened the drawstring and held up a round stone which had been carved into a skull, dark green with bands of turquoise, and shiny.

It must be the same type of stone as the skull in the outer room of the tent, in miniature. "She gave you a rock? Weird. She gave me a journal." I showed her the thin book. What kind of journal had so few pages?

Her thumb rubbed the surface of the crystal. "Well, technically a rock, but this is smooth and polished, and feels good when I rub it."

I held out my hand. "Let me feel."

Mallory took a step back and shook her head. "No, I'm sorry, Angela. Madame Vadoma told me not to let anyone else touch it."

My hand dropped. "Oh, she didn't say anything like that about the journal." I fanned through the thin book; it'd be full in a couple days. Except for the leather cover, chintzy.

"Oh, no." I snapped my fingers.

"What?"

"We have to go back." Dread settled in the pit of my stomach. "I didn't pay Madame Vadoma, did you?"

Mallory's hand flew to her mouth. "I forgot."

"I expected her to ask for the money first." Steeling myself, I turned around. Especially since she gave us gifts, we couldn't stiff her.

The tent was gone.

The cat sat on the spot where the tent had been, watching us. I blinked a few times. Still no tent past the booths. *Where did it go?*

Mallory and I exchanged a confused look.

Her eyebrows rose. "How ...?"

I shrugged. "I don't know."

"You two want to move on or move over? You're blocking traffic."

Startled, I whipped my head around. "Sorry." The word was out before I realized we'd been told off by a clown.

The clown leaned down to a little girl and asked if she wanted a giraffe. Then he pulled balloons out of his pocket and started blowing.

How rude. I get that we were blocking the aisle, but then he did the *same thing*. Just like an adult ... all *do what I say and not what I do*. Ugh.

I grabbed Mallory's arm and pulled her along. We moved between a couple booths because not as many people tried walking between them.

"What the heck?" I stared at Mallory. Her face was pale and eyes were wide. She looked as shocked as I felt. "Where did the tent go?"

She pushed her glasses firmly in place. "I don't know.

Angela, there's no way the tent could have been taken down that fast. We would have seen *something*, but there was nothing."

"I know." *Freaky.* "I didn't imagine it." Who was I trying to convince?

Mallory nodded. "Me either. We even have proof." She held up her pouch.

That's right. If the tent didn't exist, I wouldn't be clutching this journal. The journal with a spell put on it by a fortune-teller. Or maybe a curse. My stomach twisted. Curses weren't real ... were they?

"We should find the information booth so we can ask them how to pay Madame Vadoma and maybe learn something more about her."

We made our way through the crowd, then stood in line and waited our turn.

Mrs. Halverson, the school secretary, ran the information booth. "Yes, girls?"

Now that we were here, I didn't know how to start. I felt stupid saying I couldn't find a tent we left moments earlier. Saying it disappeared would be even worse. "Uh, Mrs. Halverson, we forgot to pay Madame Vadoma and don't know where she is now."

"Madame Vadoma? Who is Madame Vadoma?" Mrs. Halverson took her glasses off and let them hang from the chain around her neck.

Mallory piped up. "The fortune-teller. She told our fortunes, but we forgot to pay her."

Mrs. Halverson frowned. "I don't know what you girls are talking about. We didn't hire a fortune-teller this year. Some parents objected and we wanted to avoid any controversy."

"But we saw her and ..."

I stepped on Mallory's foot. "Thanks Mrs. Halverson. Someone must have played a joke on us. Uh, thanks, again." I pulled Mallory away from the table.

She elbowed me. "Did you have to step on my foot so hard?"

I grimaced. "Sorry. I didn't want her to ask us any questions. Mrs. Halverson should know who she booked for the carnival." I looked around us. "I feel like we entered bizarro world."

The corners of Mallory's mouth turned down. "Well, I know I wasn't dreaming. We went into a tent and we both had readings with Madame Vadoma. We even have stuff from her to prove it."

Uh oh. When she made up her mind and decided to be stubborn about it, it was like wrangling with a pit bull over a piece of meat. She never let go. "Mal, don't make a big stink about this. Do you know how strange it's going to sound to someone else?" I rubbed my hand across my eyes. "We're going to sound like a couple crazy kids making up stories."

"But what do you think happened?"

Thank goodness. For once she was going to stand down. I shrugged. "I wish I knew. Kinda spooky, don't you think?"

Mallory nodded.

"But we have to find your mom before she freaks because we're late."

When we reached Mrs. Chan by the dunk tank, her clothes were wilted from the heat. Kirky had fallen asleep in the stroller.

The faculty took turns in the dunk tank, and Vice Principal Lassiter climbed to the platform. He ran his hand over the mat of hair covering his concave chest as he got ready for the first contestant. There were things in life no student should ever see, and the Vice Principal's naked, hairy chest was one of them.

Billy Shipman, a big bruiser, took the ball, spun it in his hand then wiped the sweat from his forehead. He inhaled through his nose with a gargling sound and spit snot on the grass.

Gross.

Mr. Lassiter catcalled from inside the tank. "No arm on this one. You're gonna miss, Billy."

Billy tossed the ball up and caught it.

"What are you waiting for? The target isn't getting any bigger."

Billy's face turned red and he fired the ball. He nicked the edge of the target, but not hard enough to dunk Mr. Lassiter. He immediately fished in his wallet and paid for another chance.

"Oh too bad, Billy. Better luck this time." Mr. Lassiter swung his feet back and forth.

"You're goin' down, Lassiter." Billy threw the ball.

Missed.

"That's Mister Lassiter to you." He laughed. "Your coach

needs to spend more time with you in practice."

Billy stomped a few steps away, pounding his fist in his hand and muttering under his breath.

Zach wandered into the area and Mallory's face lit up. She nudged me.

"What?"

"No one else is in line, why don't you take a shot?"

I wiped the sweat beads off my forehead. "I don't know."

Billy stalked back and forth like a caged tiger, waiting to unleash his anger on some unsuspecting kid.

Zach waved and made straight for us ... and ran into Billy. He bounced off Billy, stumbled a couple steps back and fell on his butt.

After a quick look at Mr. Lassiter, Billy kicked dirt on Zach. "Watch where you're goin', shrimp."

Zach scrambled to his feet and dusted his shorts off.

"Where'd you get those scrawny chicken legs anyway, Taylor?" Billy tucked his thumbs into his armpits. "Bwauck. Bwauck, bwauck." He flapped his arms while scratching at the dirt with his feet. "You're just a chicken in boy form and you got the legs to prove it."

Zach's jaw set and clenched his hands into fists.

"Whatsa matter, Chicken-boy. You gonna cry?"

We needed a distraction and quick. If Zach tried to beat up Billy, he would get pulverized. All Billy had to do was sit on him.

Mallory nudged me in the side. "I'll bet if you buy three

chances, you'll get Mr. Lassiter with one of the throws." She used her best coaxing voice.

The one I always gave in to. It was odd … Mallory wouldn't say boo to a goose, except answering questions in class, and with me.

"All right. But no teasing if I miss." At least, it would stop Billy from torturing Zach.

She grinned. "Deal. But you won't miss."

I bought my chances.

"Whaddya think you're doin', Ashby?" Billy Shipman stood between me and the target, his mouth curled into a sneer.

I held the ball in front of his face. "I'm gonna throw the ball, *whaddya* think?"

Billy tried to snatch the ball as I skipped two steps to the side.

Between Billy and Cynthia it was a tight race for the biggest bully award. "What's it to you, Shipman? Is there a law that says you have to be on the baseball team?"

His nostrils flared. "You'll miss."

"Then you've got nothing to worry about. Get out of my way." I pushed him to the side.

Lassiter muffled his laughter behind his hand. "Next up, we have Angela. No arm on this one for sure. I'm going to be dry all day long."

I threw the ball and it sailed high. Missed by a mile.

Billy Shipman sniggered. "That was worse than both of mine combined. What're you gonna do for an encore?"

Cynthia joined Billy. "Good grief, Ash-can. You throw like a girl."

I had to throw twice more in front of Cynthia and Billy? If I missed again, my life was over—they'd never let me hear the end of it. I'd never forgive Mallory. I glanced over at the sidelines and she and Zach gave me a thumbs up.

"Come on Angela, you can miss again." Lassiter's smile spread.

He got a kick out of everyone missing. I didn't know whether I could put up with his smirking for two more throws. Especially if I missed.

I looked at the ground to shut out the rest of the world and the black cat from the fortune-teller tent trotted across the grass in front of me. Strange how it kept showing up.

"Quit stalling and throw, Miss Ashby."

Lassiter's smug expression made me want to knock the smile off his face.

Cynthia's braying laugh surged over everything else, and anger ignited inside me. I imagined the target was her head and threw the ball as hard as I could.

Hit. Dead Center. *Success.*

Splash. Mr. Lassiter dropped into the water and the kids nearby cheered. Except Billy and Cynthia.

"Yeah." Zach raised his arms in a victory 'V'.

As Mr. Lassiter climbed out to return to the platform, the water streamed off him. Even worse, the water caused the sunlight to glint off his graying chest hairs. I might have nightmares for weeks.

Mallory danced along the sidelines. "You've got one more chance, Angela. Get him again."

Billy's hands curled into fists and Cynthia pouted. At least they wouldn't be able to tease me on Monday.

"Beginner's luck, Angela. You'll never get me again."

"You're wrong." I wound up and threw.

Bullseye. Mr. Lassiter raised his hand to plug his nose before going under the water, but didn't do it fast enough.

I turned and walked back to Mallory, Zach, and Mrs. Chan.

"Sign that girl up for the baseball team. We need someone who can throw." Mr. Lassiter sounded half-serious.

I couldn't help myself. I peeked at Billy's face. He looked like he had a mouthful of prunes. He was supposed to be the baseball star. He took out his wallet and pulled out a wad of cash.

Now he had to try to show me up. Too bad I wasn't going to stick around and watch him.

Chapter Four - Empty House

The lights were off when we pulled up, turning the dark windows into blind eyes. I sat and stared at the empty house for a few moments, not wanting to go in. We'd stopped by Mom's work and she'd given me her credit card and a note so I could use it. She had worked out an agreement with Dad. She *promised* to be home by the time we were done.

But Mom still wasn't home from work. Unbelievable. This was *supposed* to be her day off.

Mallory nudged me.

I grabbed the bags of clothes. "Thanks for taking me shopping, Mrs. Chan."

"Thank you for helping us decide what to do with Mallory's room." She smiled. "Do you want to come to our house until your mom gets home?"

Tempted to say yes, I shook my head. "She'll be home soon. Thanks for asking, though."

After getting out of the car, I peered in at Mallory. "Have fun turning your room into a zebra haven. I have to go to my dad's tomorrow, so I'll see you on Monday. Good-bye, Kirky."

I turned to step toward the house and a small animal streaked across my path. I jumped back, hand on my chest, heart beating wildly.

A mechanism whirred, and the window slid down behind me.

"Angela, are you okay?" Mallory's voice rose as it did whenever she got a little nervous.

"Yeah, I'm fine. I just got startled by an animal." I scanned the front yard. Movement over by the side of the house caught my attention.

Dwayne rounded the corner, the bass cranked up so high, the ground beneath my feet vibrated. His headlights caught the animal's eyes and they glowed an eerie white, like an alien being. But it was just another black cat. Mrs. Hernandez must have adopted another stray.

If I were superstitious, I might be more than a little freaked out. Weren't black cats crossing your path supposed to be bad luck? Not that I believed in such guff, but seeing two of the creatures in one day seemed like a little more than coincidence. I shrugged it off.

Mrs. Chan waited at the curb until I unlocked the door and let myself in. Kirky was so cute; he kept waving until they were out of sight.

Once I closed and locked the door, I slumped against it, bags at my feet. I didn't want to move.

Dusk deepened and cast shadows across the entryway.

Tears filled my eyes and threatened to spill over. I hated my life. I spent most of my time alone. My family ripped apart.

Dad and I used to do everything together. Now I saw him once a week … if I were lucky.

I flicked the tears away, pushed off the door, and ran upstairs with my bags. If I started crying, I might not stop. Mom shouldn't have to come home to tears.

I managed to choke back my sobs while putting away my new things. Gathering the bags to throw them away, my hand curled around an object at the bottom as I tried to crumple it. Reaching inside, I pulled out the journal. *Oh yeah.* I'd tucked it in the first bag while shopping because I didn't want to carry it around, but had felt weird leaving it in the Chan's car.

Tossing the journal on my bookcase, I frowned. How *had* Madame Vadoma disappeared so quickly and completely? The journal proved we had met her.

I grabbed my math and reading books then clomped back downstairs to the kitchen to finish my homework. If I didn't, I'd have to do it at Dad's tomorrow. I tossed my books on the table as I passed on my way into the kitchen.

I stared in the fridge. Stacks of leftovers in old whipped butter containers filled the second shelf. I grabbed one from the right and peeled off the lid. The stench hit me and my head jerked back. My eyes watered from the furry contents and I quickly sealed it and put it back in the fridge.

Not willing to brave the rest of the mystery containers, I searched the other shelves. Nothing looked good. As I leaned against the wide open door, Mom's voice sounded in my head.

Shut the door. I'm not paying to refrigerate the entire kitchen.

I moved to the pantry. Nothing. All I wanted was a quick snack while I did my homework. Hopefully making a snack wouldn't turn in to making my own dinner again.

Twelve was old enough to make some simple things to eat. But I wanted Mom to be home to make dinner for me. She worked too many long hours, though. I grabbed a couple graham crackers and globbed peanut butter on them. Better than nothing and minimal cleanup. Double win.

Ugh. Stale crackers. A cracker is supposed to crunch and these were as soggy as if I'd let them sit for a couple hours after putting the peanut butter on. I sighed, poured some milk, and did my homework.

I'd just finished when Mom called to say she'd be late. *Again.*

When I took my books upstairs, my eyes traveled from the rainbow-colored graffiti wall stickers to the rainbow-striped comforter. I groaned.

Laundry. If I didn't get it done now, I'd have to do it before I could go to Dad's, and I'd have even less time to spend with him.

Stripping the bed, I carried the comforter, blankets, and sheets out to the hall, the pile so high, I couldn't see over it. My foot inched forward as I felt for the edge of the stairs.

Success. Edge found, but now what? I peered around the mass in my arms. I'd never get to the laundry room in one trip and I'd probably fall down the stairs.

Who wanted to spend all night slogging laundry up and down the stairs? The weight caused my arm to slip and I almost dropped everything.

Wait. I didn't have to carry the big bundle down. Stepping back, I wrapped the blankets tighter and tossed them.

Halfway down, they brushed the wall with a horrific scraping noise. Mom's favorite picture fell and tumbled down the stairs with the blankets. "Oh, no." *What had I done?*

I scampered down, afraid the picture had broken during the fall. I'd be in so much trouble if Mom found out.

The bedding stretched from the third stair down to the floor. I grabbed the flat sheet and gently pulled. If by some miracle the picture hadn't broken, I didn't want it to tumble out of the bedding and onto the tile.

The frame peeked out from underneath the comforter. "Please don't be broken." I grabbed the edge and closed my eyes. Mom would kill me if anything happened to this picture. Especially if she found out I'd knocked it off the wall throwing laundry down the stairs.

Phew. Not broken. A portrait of Grandma, Mom, and me taken two years ago, before Grandma passed away. I remembered sitting in one place for too long, smiling. But the picture was worth every minute.

When I put it on the hook, my heart skipped a beat. The lower-left corner was chipped.

I dashed to my room and yanked open the desk drawer.

Praying the brown felt-tip pen hadn't dried out, I snatched it and sped back to the picture. Carefully, I colored on the lighter wood so the chip didn't show quite so much.

Dad had taught me the trick of coloring wood when it got chipped. If I found the piece, I would glue it back on and the felt tip would keep the seams from showing. And if I couldn't find the piece, it might keep me out of trouble.

Shoving the pen in my back pocket, I scooped up the bedding and shuffled to the garage, taking extra care not to knock anything else off the walls or any other surface.

The bedding dropped with a *floomp* on the concrete floor. I carefully picked up each sheet and shook it, checking to see whether the chip fell out. Nothing. I repeated the process with the blanket, comforter and pillowcase.

Opening the washer, I shoved the sheets and blanket in. I eyed the washer interior. It still had more room and it would save me time on the laundry if I could get the comforter in there too.

I picked up the comforter and squished. Mostly air, so it should pack down. I twisted it like a rope and jammed it around the spindle.

Knob pulled out, soap thrown in, I dropped the lid with a clang. "Now to find the wood chip."

Cold from the tile seeped into my hands and knees as I searched. The chip shouldn't have gone far, but I didn't see it. A breeze snaked under the front door and I shivered. Mom'd been after Dad to fix it for ages. Once the sun went down, the temperature plummeted and Mom grumbled about how much it would cost to heat the house in the winter.

I spied the chip lying at the foot of the stairs, nestled up against the post. "Finally." Grabbing the wood glue from the garage, I squeezed a tiny bit onto the broken piece and pressed it into the frame.

Taking a step back, I closed my eyes and re-opened them. I couldn't see the chip. Well, if I didn't look hard for it. Hopefully, Mom would never notice.

A faint thumping noise came from the front of the house. Dwayne from three doors down must have the bass cranked up on his car stereo again. He kept the volume so loud when he drove down the street the windows on the houses shook. Mr. Hernandez would run out of the house at the first thump and yell at Dwayne to turn the music down. I don't think he realized Dwayne couldn't hear him.

I strode into the kitchen. All the panicking had made me thirsty.

As I poured some water, the thumping noise continued, getting louder with each passing moment. Between each thump came a swish. *Thump ... swish ... thump ... swish.*

Wait. Swishing? Dwayne's music never swished. The thumps came closer together.

The washing machine.

I dashed to the garage and saw it shimmying an inch at a time, getting further from the wall. I grabbed the edge and pushed, feet sliding against the floor. But it didn't move an inch backward. After a huge buck, the water hose broke loose from the washer.

"Holy crap."

The hose waved through the air spewing water full force from the end. The stream hit me in the face and I spluttered when the water went up my nose and I couldn't breathe. I stepped back and coughed. My eyes stung as I brushed the water off my face.

The washer clicked and changed from spin to rinse cycle, and the shimmying stopped. Unfortunately, it was wedged at an angle between the dryer and the freezer so I couldn't get behind it to turn off the water.

I ducked the swirling stream and ran to the washer. I pushed the knob in then leaped on top of the washer and lunged for the water valve. Leaning across the gap, I was just able to grip it.

I twisted for all I was worth, but the valve wouldn't budge. The hose got me again, and my knees slid toward the edge as I gasped and nearly slipped off.

"Power beyond my wildest imaginings, my butt." Madame Vadoma was soooo wrong. I couldn't even turn off a stupid faucet.

What if I couldn't stop the water from flooding the garage? If Mom came home before I got it all cleaned up, I'd be grounded for life.

Chapter Five - Dealing With the Aftermath

C'mon Angela, you can do this. Seizing the valve with both hands, I wrenched it as hard as I could and it finally moved. The water pressure lessened. I kept twisting until the water pressure slowed to a trickle, then stopped.

Soaked from head to toe, I turned and sat on the washer. Water dripped from my bangs into my eyes as I surveyed the damage. Except for the water covering the garage floor, nothing else seemed affected.

I hopped off the washer and grabbed Mom's rag box. "How'd this miss getting drenched?" Back on my hands and knees, I mopped up the excess water. Another load of laundry I'd have to do.

This wouldn't have happened if Mom had been home. I wouldn't have knocked the picture off, and she'd have stopped the washer before the hose spewed water everywhere. She probably would have checked to make sure I hadn't overloaded the washer to begin with.

Mom would have been home if she and Dad weren't

divorced.

Their divorce ruined my life.

After wrestling with the hose to get it back on the washer, and moving things around inside, I started it again. I held my breath hoping the hose would stay on as the water filled the tub. When it began to swish, I left.

I stopped at the door. If I dripped water through the house, I'd have another mess to clean up. Stripping, I tossed my wet clothes by the washer, wrapped a dry towel from the rag box around me, and fled to the stairs leaving no sign of the disaster except damp footsteps on the tile.

Showered, changed, and wet clothes in the wash, I made it back to the family room and plopped on the couch to watch TV. I listened as car after car passed on the street, and one finally pulled into the drive. I glanced at the clock. Almost eight o'clock, again.

The door swung open and Mom entered, her arms full of bags. "Hey, Ange. A little help?"

I grabbed a bag before it fell from her arms and took it to the kitchen.

Once she put the sacks on the counter, she hugged me. "How was your day, sweetie?"

I shrugged. "It was okay." Definitely not the time to mention the washer fiasco and I would never talk about the picture. I scuffed my toe against the floor. "It would have been better if you'd been with me."

Mom stroked my hair and grimaced. "I'm sorry, hon."

Disappointed, I scowled. "But you were supposed to go with me to the school carnival." We never had time to do anything together any more. Add another way the divorce ruined my life.

She laughed. "No one wants to go with their mom …" Her eyes met mine and the smile died on her lips. "Oh, honey. Please don't take it so hard. I'll make it up to you."

Yeah, right. How could she make it up to me when she was never home to begin with? I stalked away and flopped on the plush cinnamon love seat. I picked at the rope coming through on the corners.

"Angela, can I get you to help me put the groceries away, please?"

I groaned.

Her hand flew to her hip. "Angela, I'm tired. I don't have the strength or energy to deal with attitude tonight."

"F-i-i-i-i-ne." I dragged myself from the couch and stomped to the kitchen.

Neither of us said a word as I grabbed a bag, pulled a package of spaghetti out, and set it on the counter. I rubbed the tile surface with the tips of my fingers. I'd shopped with Dad for the tile because he wanted to surprise Mom with a new countertop. He had been so excited when he found the white tile with rainbow iridescent swirls because he knew Mom would be ecstatic.

Mom plugged the kettle in for cocoa.

Did she remember how hard he'd worked to install the

counter for her? She hadn't even complained about the mess he'd made with the grout.

Mom held up a can of *Moos Chocolate Whipped Cream.* "Do you want whipped cream on top?"

I shrugged. "Okay, I guess."

Mom bit her lip.

I put the last box in the pantry as the water boiled. Mom poured the water on the cocoa mix and the chocolaty aroma filled the kitchen. I danced around shaking the whipped cream, while Mom stirred and added a touch of milk.

She tapped the spoon on the rim. "Okay, spray me."

I pointed the nozzle at her and cocked an eyebrow. "Really?"

"No." Her hands flew up in front of her. "Just hit the cocoa."

I put big, fluffy clouds of whipped cream on each cup, then put the end in my mouth and gave a squirt.

"Angela! How many times have I told you about putting the nozzle in your mouth?"

I grinned and a dollop of whipped cream squeezed out the corner. I wiped it with my thumb and sucked it off. "I stopped counting."

"Oh Angela, don't be silly. Why don't you make some popcorn?"

Mom was going all out to make up for not being able to go to the carnival with me. I threw a popcorn bag into the microwave and set the timer. I loved the popping sound when the kernels burst. And there was nothing like the smell of fresh popcorn. When the popping finished, I poured the bag into two bowls and set them on the table.

I carried my cup over. Before setting it down, I flicked my tongue across the top and let the chocolaty cream melt in my mouth.

Mom sat and laced her fingers around her cup. "Angela, we need to talk about how you're dealing with the divorce."

Not again. Mentally I groaned, but didn't make the mistake of letting it out.

When I didn't say anything, Mom sighed. "You've had to make some big adjustments because I'm working so many hours. And it may feel like it's always going to be this way, but it won't be." She waited for me to speak.

I stirred the whipped cream into the cocoa, my lips pressed tightly together.

She took a sip, and a brown speck covered the tip of her nose. "You know I'm searching for a better job, with more pay and fewer hours, but right now, this is what I have."

The whipped cream on her nose made mine tickle. "Uh, Mom? You might want to …" I brushed my nose.

She pinched the tip of her nose, looked at her fingers, and laughed. "Thank you." She scrubbed her nose with a napkin.

"If you need to talk to a counselor about your feelings, your dad and I will make sure you get the help you need."

I grabbed a handful of popcorn. "Mom, I'm fine. I don't need to talk to anyone."

Mom stared at me for a long moment, concern wrinkling her brow. "Well, if you're sure. Anytime you change your mind, you let me know." She placed some popcorn on her napkin. "So tell me all about the carnival and then I want to see your new clothes."

We spent the rest of the night chatting like old times and I modeled my new clothes.

As Mom left my room, she paused at the door and leaned against the jamb. "I've missed this so much, Angela. I like spending time with you." Her fingers trailed the door, lingering as she left.

Chapter Six - Disappointment

Sunlight streamed through the curtains and hit my eyes. Traces of my dreams hung around a moment before breaking up and disappearing like smoke. Except for being about a black cat with glowing eyes, I couldn't remember anything. I laughed. The cat from last night had invaded my dreams. I pulled my comforter higher to block the light. But it was no use. Not able to go back to sleep, I stretched and rolled to look at the clock.

Noon? But I never slept in.

My stomach clenched. Something must be wrong. Dad should have been here to pick me up already.

It's a good thing I had done all my chores because Mom wouldn't let me go if they weren't. If I wasn't ready to go, it'd be one more thing for them to fight about.

Yanking my comforter over the pillow, I smoothed out the lumps. I shoved my feet in my slippers and hurried to the bathroom.

Showered, changed, and hair curling from the steam, I ran

down the stairs. Mom sat at the kitchen table with papers strewn all over.

Her eyes looked tired above her smile. "I wondered how long you'd sleep."

"I'm sorry. I didn't mean to sleep so late." My stomach growled. I'd have to eat before I did anything. "When is Dad supposed to be here?" I needed to know how fast I had to move.

The hurt in Mom's eyes said it all. "Angela."

"Don't." He wasn't coming, but I didn't want to hear her say it. No wonder she let me sleep in.

I tore up the stairs, leaped onto the bed, and buried my head in the pillow.

Not even a minute later, I heard Mom's footsteps along the hall. "Honey."

"Leave me alone." I didn't want to hear whatever lame excuse Dad had given her for not wanting to spend time with me.

She tapped on the door before opening it.

Lifting my head, I glared at Mom as she crept into the room. "Is this what I'm supposed to deal with because of the divorce?" I turned to face the wall. "Yeah. I'll work on making sure I don't care anymore."

"Angela, sweetie, I'm so sorry." The bed creaked as she sat on the edge and rubbed my back. "Your dad cares about you—"

"Yeah, right. He cares so much he can't bother to spend time with me. The only one he cares about is Holly. I *hate* her."

Mom took a deep breath. "Ange, something unavoidable came up."

The anger burning in the pit of my stomach swelled. "Don't lie to me. I don't fit in his new life with Holly-the-homewrecker and he doesn't want the hassle." Tears brimming, I faced her. "Please, just leave me alone."

Her forehead wrinkled and frown deepened, but she stood and left the room.

I flopped onto my back and stared at the ceiling. I should get used to being forgotten by Dad. Who could blame him for not wanting me around?

When Dad and I spent time together, I was a living reminder to his new wife Holly that she wasn't the first love of Dad's life. And I never made any attempt to get along with her. She tried to be nice to me, but only because she wanted to make Dad think she was perfect. So I did my best to be a pain in her side because she ruined my life.

The scene I had caused the last time I had been with them rolled in my head.

I stuffed my history book into the backpack and zipped it up. Before grabbing the handle, I took a look around my sometime bedroom to see whether I had forgotten anything. I sneered. Talk about the least inviting place. Holly had *decorated* it for me.

Off-white walls, standard issue floral curtains and

matching bedspread, the room could have been designed for a hotel. It certainly wasn't something a nearly teenaged girl wanted. No personality at all. *Boring.*

So, yeah, it wasn't *my* bedroom at my dad's, it was the guest room and I just happened to be the one who occupied it most frequently.

Despite having all my things, I stood in the middle of the room, stuck. I wanted to spend the last few minutes of the weekend with Dad, but Holly would be there. We couldn't even go out to his workshop and build stuff like we used to without her interrupting us.

"Angela?"

I cringed. Just the sound of her mousy voice sent shudders through me.

The door creaked open and Holly poked her head through the opening. "Do you have all your things? I thought we could leave a little early and stop somewhere along the way for a bite to eat. Your pick."

"What's the matter? Did the Internet run out of tasty recipes you can fail at in under thirty minutes?"

The flush creeped up her throat into her face until it glowed a bright red. "I … I meant it as a treat since we don't ever go out to eat as a family."

Family. The word sucker-punched me in the gut. Family is what I used to have before *she* came along. "Fine. Let's go to Famous Dave's for a burger."

I wanted to go to the Italian place over on 3rd Street, but

Mom, Dad, and I had been there too often as a family, and it felt wrong.

"But I thought we might—" Holly's lips pinched tight at my glare.

I held back a laugh. Dave's was only famous in the mind of the owner, Dave. But it was the perfect place for Holly, who detested burgers, and wouldn't find a single salad on the menu. If we were going to eat as a *family*, she'd have to sacrifice her precious waistline.

Although, by the looks of it, she may have been secretly hitting the burgers. Her *oh-so-petite* frame wasn't quite so petite any more. What had she been doing to pack on the pounds?

I swung the backpack over my shoulder and strode toward the door. Dad stood in the den sneaking in a few minutes watching football before we left.

"Game good?"

"Hey, Pumpkin." He put his arm across my shoulders.

Before he had a chance to bore me about the game, Holly grabbed the remote and turned off the set. Then she put her arms around us both, and bowed her head.

"Let's pray. Dear Heavenly Father, I ask …"

What the—

I broke from her embrace. "I'm going to the car." It was all I could do to keep from yelling at her.

I didn't want her to touch me, let alone hug me. And in prayer? If I needed to pray, I'd do it one on one with God. When I reached the car, I opened the back door, threw my backpack in, slid in after it, and slammed the door.

A few minutes later, Dad and Holly followed me out. Holly dabbed her eyes with a tissue, then blew her nose.

After getting in the car, Dad turned and gazed at me, his eyes boring into mine, the pain in them pinning me to the back seat. "You ready?"

I gave him a curt nod and he turned away as if he couldn't bear to look at me for another second. Heaviness settled in my heart as he started the car.

Holly's periodic sniffs were the only sound on our way to Dave's. Did she have to be such a dramatic diva? But if I said anything, Dad would be even more annoyed.

So much for going out to eat as a treat.

The aroma of frying burgers and onions greeted us when Dad opened the door at Famous Dave's. I told him what I wanted to eat and sat in a booth next to the window. Holly followed and slid into the booth on the opposite side of the table. She cupped her hand over her mouth and nose and her face paled to the point where it took on a slightly green tinge. Our eyes met and hers welled with tears. I stared out the window. *Can this visit just be over already?*

If I had to keep staring out the window to avoid Holly's suffocating sorrow, I'd get a crick in my neck. And it wasn't like anything interesting was happening. Cars zoomed by on the road and an old guy walking his dog stopped every few steps to let his dog sniff stuff and then pee on it. *Gross.*

When Dad carried the food to the table, he put my burger

down in front of me with a bang and sat next to Holly.

He wouldn't speak to me. He was upset, but it wasn't my fault. I jabbed a french fry in ketchup and shoved it in my mouth. I glanced at Holly.

She pressed her lips together and her chin trembled.

For goodness sake. Not tears again.

She dashed the tear away as it fell and Dad patted her hand.

How did I get to be the bad guy in all this? It wasn't fair. I refused to look at Dad. I didn't want to see the disappointment on his face. How did Holly do it? She was the one who should apologize. I never asked for her to hug me. Besides, group hugs were for sporting events. I wolfed my food down as fast as I could. I wanted to go home.

Chapter Seven - First Entry

I punched my pillow. Dad probably called off my visit because he didn't want a repeat of last time. I had never told Mom what happened. The whole thing embarrassed me because I felt so weird about it.

For once, I hadn't gone out of my way to hurt Holly. Normally, I took every opportunity I could to put Holly down in front of Dad. But this time, I hadn't. I wasn't prepared for the hug and it made me angry. I couldn't explain. Not even to myself.

As for the other times, I don't know what I thought. Maybe that if he saw I didn't like her, Dad would come to his senses and come back to Mom.

Things used to be good. We had a lot of laughs together, and they did love each other. Before. But right before Dad left, they did nothing but argue.

They argued even more now.

Mom's voice floated up the stairway. She must've called Dad and they were arguing again. But this time I knew what it was about.

Me.

I felt worse when she badgered Dad about upsetting me. He knew he had, and when she argued with him about it, he loved me even less.

Tears threatened to spill over again. I needed something to distract me. My gaze fell on the journal.

Maybe Madame Vadoma knew what she was talking about. My heart felt so full, maybe writing down my feelings would make things better. I grabbed the book and sat at my desk. The plain cover had the word *Journal* embossed in gold on the front. I inhaled the leather scent and felt calmer.

I opened it to the front page. My eyes bugged out. *The Journal of Angela Ashby* was inscribed in thick black ink. Underneath were the words Madame Vadoma told me, '*Use it wisely.*'

How was my name in the journal? It freaked me out. I had never once mentioned my name to Madame Vadoma, and even if she had listened to Mallory and me in the tent while we waited for her, she wouldn't have known my last name. I wanted to call Mallory and tell her about the inscription, but remembered Mom was on the phone with Dad. Arguing.

I turned the page and took out my favorite purple pen. I stopped for a moment. I didn't know exactly how a journal worked. I didn't want to put *Dear Diary*—too lame. And this wasn't a diary.

I closed my eyes and tried to remember what Madame

Vadoma told me.

Write what was in my heart. But how? I had so many feelings swirling inside, I didn't know where to start. I couldn't concentrate with the occasional raised voice penetrating my door. I loved my parents and I didn't want them to hate each other. Especially because of me.

I grabbed my MP3 player and shoved the headphone buds in my ears. I took a deep breath and sighed. Sometimes blocking out the world was the only thing to do.

My hand hovered over the page. I took a deep breath and pressed the pen to the page.

> I hope I'm doing this right. But I got this journal from a creepy fortune-teller who disappeared, so I can't ask anyone.

I paused to think about what I felt in my heart before scribbling more in the journal. Thoughts of Dad, Holly, Mom, and how things had changed since the divorce churned in my head. So many things I wanted to gripe about, but I didn't want to turn the journal into a complaint book. What if Mom found it? She'd be so hurt. She had been hurt enough already. And it was all Holly's fault for taking Dad away.

I closed my eyes and listened to the music. Holding the pen like a drumstick, I beat time with the music on my desk. Then I knew. Without trying to think about what was most important to me, it just popped into my head.

I'm tired of coming home to an empty house and having to get my own dinner and spending so much time on my own. Since I can't undo the divorce, I want Mom to be able to stay home with me, so we can spend more time together.

The simple words drying on the page choked me. The purple ink imbued the words with a power I couldn't describe. I had written what I wanted most. But vibrations came from the journal, mostly good, but an underlying darkness grew. I closed the journal and put it back on the bookcase. *Good grief. I was getting as superstitious as Mallory.* Maybe journaling wasn't the best idea after all.

Another Monday come and gone. Mallory and I made our way to the front of the school to go home. Jimmy Simmons and his friends ran past, playing tag and calling each other names. Mallory flung a wistful look toward the bike racks where Zach twirled the dial on his bike lock.

"Race you to the postbox." I hitched my backpack tighter.

"Go."

We took off running down the street, side by side, sneakers pounding the sidewalk. My Saint Christopher necklace slipped out of my shirt and bounced against my chest as we tore around kids on their way home. I glanced at Mallory.

She looked determined to beat me. Her hair flew out behind her like a shiny, black flag. Spotting a skateboard in time, I leaped over it while Mallory dodged a ramp. The Miller kids always left something out on the sidewalk.

Uh-oh. Toddler riding a foot-powered car straight ahead. Veering off the sidewalk, I went over the curb and ran along the dry gutter and Mallory took to the green-belt. Neither of us wanted to get yelled at by the kid's mom for running too close to him. Once past the toddler, we converged on the sidewalk again, footsteps thumping in time with my heart.

At the park, we both cut across the grass, shaving the corner off our route. My feet squelched through the section they always overwatered. I skirted the kids' jungle gym while Mallory ploughed through the sand. Hitting the sidewalk again on the far side of the park, we sprinted down the straightaway. A black cat sauntered across the sidewalk and sat in front of the postbox. I slowed for a moment. Why did that cat keep showing up?

My lungs burned as I put on the final spurt of speed to beat Mallory to the postbox by two steps. I stretched my hand out and touched the blue painted metal as I flew past.

My steps slowed and I went back to where she stood, hanging on the postbox, panting.

"I almost … beat you … that time." She wiped the beads of sweat from her brow.

I used my sleeve to mop my face. The salt in the sweat stung my eyes. "You're getting faster." I slowly inhaled to help ease the stitch in my side. "You ready?"

She nodded and we walked toward home, the cat following behind. Who did it belong to?

I tucked the medal back in my shirt. I smiled; Mom wanted me to wear the Saint Christopher to help keep me safe. She said she needed all the help she could get.

My backpack hung from one shoulder as I trudged home after saying good-bye to Mallory. I turned the corner onto my street and grinned. Mom's car sat in the driveway. For *once* she wasn't going to be late. I broke into a run.

Chapter Eight - The Journal

Bursting through the front door, I opened my mouth to call out. The words froze in my throat. Mom sat at the kitchen table, crying. My backpack hit the ground with a thud.

She raised her tear-stained face. "I got laid off today. They told me I was doing a great job, but they had to make some cuts to stay in business." She choked back a sob. "What are we going to do?"

My feet unstuck from where they were glued to the floor and I ran and threw my arms around her. "You'll find another job."

She hugged me so tight my ribs hurt.

"I hope so, honey. You know I've been trying. Jobs are scarce right now." She took a deep breath, released me and grabbed a napkin to wipe her face. "But you don't need to worry. I'll get something. We'll be okay."

I sighed. Mom always told me to focus on the positive, so she had to set the example. But she didn't believe it. At least not yet.

"Do you want me to make dinner?"

Mom raised her eyebrow. "And what delicacy are you planning to serve?"

I shrugged. "Well, I make a mean peanut butter graham cracker."

Mom snorted. "Why don't you close the front door before we have every stray cat in the neighborhood taking up residence in our living room? And I'll make us something to eat."

At least I made her laugh.

A bubble of happiness warred with the fear inside me. It was terrible that Mom had lost her job, but she'd have more time to spend with me until she got a new one.

After dinner, I washed the dishes with no argument. "Do you want to watch a movie?"

Mom looked up from the paper, where she'd circled several want ads. "I can't. I have to keep looking for jobs." She patted the laptop on the table next to her. "Once I go through the paper, I have to get this cranked up and see what else I can find."

"That stinks. You can't even take a couple hours to relax?"

She shook her head. "I can't stop until I have another job, hon."

I slumped on the couch and put my feet on the coffee table. So much for spending more time with her.

"Angela, take your feet off the table. You know better." Mom pursed her lips. "Have you finished your homework?"

"No." I huffed, rolled off the couch, and stomped toward the stairs.

I flung the bedroom door open and threw my backpack on the bed.

After pulling my history book out of the bag, I sat at the desk and cracked the pages. Why did history books have to be so boring? Exciting stuff happened, but you'd never know it from our history book. I think they forgot the *story* part of history.

A bland recital of facts and dates, 'The Pandora myth first appears in lines 560–612 of Hesiod's poem ...,' blah, blah, blah. The tedium caused my eyes to glaze. I couldn't believe this book made Greek mythology boring. We were reading about Pandora, which should have been exciting. It would have made a great movie. The special effects when she broke open the box would be awesome.

I closed the history book. I wasn't in the mood, and I had until Wednesday to finish. I grabbed my math book. I scribbled down the answers to the two problems I had left. Math homework complete, I pulled out my English homework.

About halfway through, I closed the book. I couldn't concentrate on anything. Mom said not to worry about what would happen to us, but I couldn't help it.

Mom did her best, but since Dad left, money had been tight. She had never said anything, but any time I needed something for school the grooves between her eyebrows deepened in pain. Maybe I should take back some of my new clothes.

Remembering her tears made me shaky inside. I didn't

know what I'd do if Mom crumbled. She always held us together. My heart jolted. Would we have to sell the house and move?

My gaze traveled around the room. The wild psychedelic print on the wall Mom and I picked out together. The stair step bookcase Dad and I sanded and varnished together. My grandmother's hope-chest at the foot of the bed, where I kept all my treasures.

This had always been my room. I didn't want to move into a strange house and have to get used to a new room.

Every well-worn and loved object had memories attached. My eyes stopped on the journal. The newest thing I owned, except for my clothes. A twinge of guilt pricked my conscience. It bugged me we hadn't been able to pay Madame Vadoma for the reading. What if the journal was cursed because I hadn't paid?

She gave it to me though, and didn't ask for any money.

I closed my eyes to block the journal out. A vision of Madame Vadoma handing it to me rose in my mind's eye. Her intense stare as she told me to use it wisely increased. Until all I "saw" was her glare. My eyes flew open.

Journaling hadn't made me feel better last time, but maybe I needed to give it a chance.

Seeing my name in the angular, foreign-looking script still shocked me. I had forgotten to tell Mallory about the name at the front. I turned the page. My words from yesterday mocked me.

I got what I wanted, but at what price? I didn't want Mom to lose her job. What had gone wrong?

Madame Vadoma said I had to use it with a pure heart. Maybe what I had written was too selfish. I only thought about what I wanted. Settling in at my desk, I turned the page. Maybe I should try again.

Sometimes getting what you want isn't the best thing in the world. Mom is home tonight, so I should be happy, right? But when she's crying because she lost her job, happiness seems kinda far away. If I could go back to yesterday and do it over, I wouldn't want Mom to stay home with me. I'd want her to have a better job, making more money, but not have to work such long hours. Then we could both be happy.

I picked up the journal. Did I need to add anything else? A gentle rumble rippled through the journal—like holding a purring kitten. But journals don't purr, so my hands must be shaking. I reread the words on the page.

What the heck? The entry read like I believed what I wrote yesterday made Mom lose her job. *Ridiculous.* I looked at the journal. Plain lined paper covered in leather. Nothing special.

Madame Vadoma must have bewitched me into thinking the journal had special powers. All the talk about the heart having power and using it wisely. Any connection to what I had written and what happened to Mom was coincidence. Nothing more. Otherwise it meant I had caused an entire company to fail.

I giggled. No twelve-year-old had that kind of power.

What would Mom say if I told her that what I wrote in the journal came true? She'd probably talk about having me see someone because of the divorce again.

I closed the journal and stared at it. Nothing. No glow. No vibrations.

Well ... I wriggled my shoulders. The memory of last night's vibrations and the darkness creeping out from the pages made me uncomfortable. I shoved the memory down—nothing more than an overactive imagination.

Its pages didn't call my name, or pull me inside. And the ink didn't disappear into the page. And except for my name at the front, no one else's writing was in it. Kinda tame for a magical object. In fact, it looked and acted exactly like a journal.

Which is exactly what it was. And a pretty measly one at that.

Moving it to the side, I went back to my English homework. Maybe writing in it did work, because I felt a little better.

"Angela!"

Mom's voice penetrated the mists of my dream. Morning already?

"Angela, get up."

I couldn't be late for school already. The light through the window barely lit the room. And Mom sounded happy and not angry.

Shoving my feet into my slippers, I dashed to the door.

Mom just missed hitting me as she burst through it. "I got a call from a job I interviewed for *months* ago, and they want to make me an offer."

My eyes widened and my jaw dropped. "Really?" The word trailed up into a squeak.

She hugged me. "This is the job I wanted, too. It's with a good, established company and the benefits are wonderful." She swung me around. "I can't tell you how happy I am. I'd given up hope they'd call. And that they called on the day after I lost my other job makes it sweeter."

The big smile on my face made my cheeks hurt, but I couldn't stop. "I am so excited for you. When do you start?"

Mom's eyes danced with happiness. "I'm going in today to do the preliminary paperwork, and they want me to start immediately."

"Yay!"

"So you need to get ready for school. I'll drop you off a bit early, if that's okay."

"Sure."

Mom grinned. "I'll get breakfast ready while you get dressed."

I rushed through my morning routine and clomped down the stairs, as Mom finished making breakfast. Fried egg and turkey bacon sandwich on toasted English muffin. My favorite.

Mom sat at the table with me to drink her coffee while I ate. I couldn't remember the last time we had breakfast together.

She took a sip from the steaming cup. "Did you finish your homework last night?"

I nodded and only felt a pinch of guilt. I didn't finish the history homework. But it wasn't due until tomorrow, so technically it became tonight's homework.

I took a bite of my sandwich and savored it; the crunch of the bacon and the squish of the egg both cushioned by the muffin. Mom got the yolk perfect—cooked, but creamy liquid to soak into the muffin crannies. I closed my eyes as I chewed. "Mmmmm."

Mom laughed. "I'm glad you enjoy your food."

"It's the best, because …"

She joined me.

"… it's made with love."

Done with breakfast, I pounded upstairs to grab my books. Still stacked on my desk from last night, I shoved them into my backpack and ran back downstairs.

Chapter Nine – Gnome Outside the Window

Sitting on the planter ledge in the middle of the quad, I pulled out my history book. I might as well get the boring reading done. A shadow crossed the page as I flipped it.

I glanced up. Cynthia.

I didn't get it. She didn't like me, so why didn't she just stay away? Instead, she sought me out and picked fights. A big bully and I didn't give in to bullying.

I stared at her, hoping she'd go away. She didn't. Movement over by the lockers caught my attention. A black cat slunk along the lockers, then disappeared around the corner of the building.

"What are you doing here so early, Ash-Angel?" Cynthia sneered at me.

What did that even mean? I ignored her and went back to reading.

"You know what an Ash-Angel is? The opposite of a snow angel. Instead of sparkly white, it's filthy."

Not looking up, I shrugged. "That's lame." Didn't she

know if she had to force it, it didn't work?

Her shadow loomed when she took a step forward. "Watch it, Be-Ash."

I closed my history book and slowly clapped my hands. "Congratulations on coming up with a new insult, even if it's just switching the syllables of my last name around. I'll bet your parents are proud."

She frowned and curled her fists.

"But you'd better be careful who you use it around. After all, a teacher might think you're saying something else." Inhaling sharply, I covered my mouth in mock dismay. "Then you might have to explain how you came up with such an endearing nickname." I opened the history book again.

Cynthia knocked the book to the ground. "You'd better be careful, Ash-can. There's no one around to save your sorry butt."

"Awww, you've already gone back to the same old boring name-calling." I exaggerated a pout. "And—pbbbt—I've never needed anyone to save my butt, especially from you." Maybe I shouldn't have made the farting noise, but she was getting on my nerves.

Retrieving the book from the ground, I opened it again. From the look on her face, Cynthia might erupt this time.

She cocked her arm back, and I got ready to duck. With any luck she'd drive herself into the planter.

Mrs. Clark passed us. "Good morning, ladies." She wore a black skirt, with a red blazer over a crisp white blouse that almost glowed against her dark skin.

Cynthia's arm dropped to her side.

"Morning, Mrs. Clark." We both said the words at the same time.

Cynthia glared at me like she was the only one who had the right to talk. I wasn't going to put up with that.

Out of the corner of my eye, I checked for Mrs. Clark. She stood in the same place and pretended to read her notebook while keeping her eye on us. "Why don't you go pick on someone your own size?" I lowered my voice so only Cynthia would hear. "Oh, that's right. King Kong doesn't go to this school."

Mallory was right. I couldn't stop baiting her. It was too much fun.

Her face into a giant snarl. "Watch your back Ash-can. 'Cause when no one is around, I'm gonna grind your butt into the ground like a cigarette."

Slapping the page of the book, I let out a fake laugh. "I totally get it ... cigarette butt, Ash-can ... you're such a wit." I turned the page. "A dimwit." The last words were said under my breath because I didn't have a death wish.

Cynthia glowered at me, but turned and stomped off.

Even she wasn't stupid enough to hit me with a teacher watching.

The quad filled with the chatter of students, so school would start soon.

I decided not to wait for Mallory because I didn't want to give Cynthia another opportunity to attack. Gathering my things, I headed to class. On my way, I passed Mrs. Clark. She was the best. She let us listen to the radio during class and if we got our work done, we didn't have to be quiet all the time.

She waved me over. "Angela, may I have a word?"

"Yes, Mrs. Clark."

She took off her glasses and tucked them in the v-neck of her blouse and her brown eyes pierced mine. "The girl who kicks the hornets' nest usually gets stung."

My cheeks flushed. "Yes, Mrs. Clark. I'll ... I'll remember."

She patted my shoulder. "Good. Now off to class with you."

I'd messed up in front of my favorite teacher. *Way to go, Angela!*

I slunk into homeroom, and took my seat.

Plunking my backpack down next to my chair, I avoided Mrs. Clark's eye, embarrassed by our earlier encounter. I pulled my English book out from the backpack. A light thud followed as the journal fell to the ground. *Oops.* I meant to leave it at home, but must have grabbed it with the other books on the desk.

Mrs. Clark called the class to order. I shoved the journal under my English book.

Fifteen minutes before the end of class, Mrs. Clark stopped lecturing. "I refuse to compete with the lunch bell for attention.

Free reading and writing time."

I thought about reading, but decided to journal about Cynthia and her bullying instead.

When I opened the pages and reread last night's entry, I got a funny feeling in my stomach, as if a dozen butterflies were playing tackle football in there. In my first entry, I wrote about wanting Mom to stay home and she lost her job. Last night I wrote about her getting a better job, and this morning her dream company called with one.

Coincidence?

It had to be … didn't it?

I couldn't get the idea out of my head that somehow writing in the journal caused both things to happen. But how could I prove it?

I stared out the window at the bushes and trees behind our building. Inspiration dawned.

Pen gripped so tightly my fingers turned white, my hand hovered over the page. Should I try?

I shrugged. What did I have to lose? I relaxed my grip a bit and wrote.

> It would be cool if a gnome would appear in the bushes outside my English class.

I stared at the words for a moment and then stared out the window. Nothing.

Disappointment surged through me. What did I expect anyway? Like a gnome would really pop out of the bushes and wave at me. I slouched in my chair and tapped the pen against the journal. Wanting the journal to have power was nothing more than wishful thinking.

A movement outside caught my eye.

I blinked.

A little man with a full white beard, and fluffy eyebrows, wearing a blue work shirt, sat in the middle of the grass outside the window and waved at me. He didn't have the red pointed hat I expected, but a flat cap covered his head instead. His face, lined with the wrinkles of a lifetime, wore a gleeful expression.

I shook my head and blinked again.

He remained sitting cross-legged, his big round cheeks pink, and a twinkle in his eye to beat my dad's. Then—poof. He disappeared.

The bell signaling lunchtime rang.

Had I really seen a gnome out the window? Or was it a short old man? My backpack on the desk, I tried to put the English book in, but it slid off and hit the desk. I stared out the window. Everything looked just as it had before the gnome appeared. The book hit the desk again.

"Hey, Ashby."

I tore my gaze from the window.

Joaquin Ortega erupted in a fit of laughter. "It might work better if you unzip it first."

My face flushed so hot, I was surprised I didn't have flames dancing on my cheeks. "Uh, thanks." Now would be a good time for an earthquake fault to open beneath my feet and suck me in. Once I unzipped the pack, I finally put the books away.

I *had* to find Mallory. Once I told her what happened with Mom's job and the gnome, she'd look me straight in the eye and tell me to quit dreaming. The journal was something to write thoughts in. Nothing more.

I found her at the lunch tables. *Who could think about eating at a time like this?*

Mallory scooted to make room for me at the table. "What's the matter, Ange? You look like you're in shock."

The tables were full and kids yelled to one another across the lunch area, while others milled about searching for a place to sit. "Uh, Mal? Do you think we can go somewhere a little quieter?"

I wanted to share the coincidences of the journal with Mallory, not with half the middle school. Besides, everyone else might think I'd lost my mind.

And I wasn't sure I hadn't.

Mallory gathered her things. "Is it good, Angela?"

I tugged on her elbow. "I don't think you'll have any cause to complain."

I dragged Mallory out to the athletic field. I didn't know whether the gnome would show up out here. But there would be fewer kids to overhear our conversation. And we'd see anyone coming before they'd hear us.

"Remember the journal Madame Vadoma gave me?"

Mallory rolled her eyes. "Since it was two days ago, yes, I can remember back that far."

"You didn't tell her my name, did you?"

She shook her head.

"It's weird because the first time I opened the journal, my name was already inside. My *full* name."

Mallory's eyebrows rose.

"Have you … um … used the rock she gave you?"

"I don't know about *used*, but I have looked up what it is. It's a malachite crystal and I've been doing a little research on what it means and what I'm supposed to do with it." Mallory sat cross-legged on the basketball court and opened her lunch. "What does my crystal have to do with anything?"

A pair of amber eyes peered at us from the bushes on the edge of the athletic field. The black cat must have recently moved into the neighborhood. Up until the carnival, I had never seen it, but I'd seen it four or five times around the school since. I sat next to Mallory. "Have you noticed anything strange about it?

"No." Mallory sounded a tiny bit exasperated. "Angela, get to the point."

I took a deep breath. "I-think-what-I-write-in-my-journal-comes-true." The words all ran together, but at least I said them.

"What?" Mallory held up her hand. "Wait. What are you talking about, Angela?"

With a shaking hand, I pulled the journal out of my backpack. "Look." I pointed to the first entry.

"Geez, your writing looks like chicken scratch. How am I supposed to read it?"

What? I glanced at the journal. I didn't have the best handwriting in the world, but it was legible. "Are you going blind?" I shoved the journal in front of her nose.

"Weird. It looks fine now." Her nose wrinkled.

"After I wrote that, my mom lost her job."

Mallory shrugged. "Coincidence."

"I know, but the next night I wrote this." I pointed to the entry where I wished my mom would get a better job. "She got the call this morning and was offered a job."

Mallory rubbed her chin. "But your mom has been applying for jobs for a little while now, hasn't she?"

I nodded. "I thought the whole thing was coincidence too, but during English, I tested it. Read the next entry."

Mallory's glasses slid down her nose as she read. "You are *not* going to tell me a gnome showed up behind the English building."

I didn't say anything.

"Seriously? Okay. Prove it."

"But how do I prove it? The gnome disappeared after a few minutes." I couldn't believe I was having this conversation.

Mallory stared at the ground for a moment. Then a smile lit her face. "I know. Make a unicorn run around the track."

Chapter Ten - The Unicorn and the Fairy

My eyes bulged and I stared at Mallory as the idea seized me. The gnome could have been any old short man, but a unicorn … if a unicorn ran across the field, it had to be the journal.

I grabbed my pen and without hesitation began to write.

> Mallory and I were talking about how fantastic it would be to see a unicorn run around the track. I'd love to see one up close. Are they like a horse, but with a single horn? or are they magical?

As soon as I finished, Mallory looked out at the track. "See? Nothing there."

A little disappointed, I kept searching for the unicorn anyway. "It took a couple minutes for the gnome to appear, so maybe there's a delay factor."

Mallory snorted and opened her mouth, but never uttered a word.

Hooves pounded the ground.

I jumped to my feet and scanned the field, searching for the source of the hoof beats. I'd be so disappointed if it turned out to be someone riding a horse past the school.

But there, galloping down the track, mane and beard streaming from its neck and head, was the most beautiful white horse. Except, it wasn't a horse. A long horn protruded from the forehead and the body had a radiant quality, as if lit from the inside. It ran with perfect fluid motion.

Mallory's jaw dropped. "I don't believe my eyes."

I squealed. "I know." I bounced on the balls of my feet. "It's wonderful." I looked around to make sure we were the only ones on the athletic field.

The unicorn slowed to a halt, then beckoned us with a toss of its head.

When Mallory got to her feet, her knees trembled. Mine didn't feel all too steady, either.

She clutched my arm. "W-w-what if I d-d-d-on't want to get up close and personal with it?"

"I don't think we have a choice." I glanced at the unicorn walking toward us and nearly squealed again. Its cloven hooves clip-clopped on the ground. Definitely not a horse dressed up to look like a unicorn.

Mallory squeezed my arm even tighter. "Why don't we

have a choice?"

"I said we wanted to see it up close."

"Why did you do that?" Her voice became a high-pitched squeak.

The animal, already big from a distance, grew larger as it advanced. I caught a touch of Mallory's nerves.

Unicorns are peaceful creatures. They had to be, right? None of the myths talked about the attack of the killer unicorn. Well … not unless provoked. And we weren't going to do anything to make it angry, like trying to steal its hair or horn. Unicorns went together with rainbows, for crying out loud.

I sure hoped the myths were true. It was just much bigger than I had expected.

"Come on, Mal. This is what you wanted. Let's go meet our first-ever mythical creature." I strode toward the beast, dragging Mallory with me.

The unicorn stopped when we approached.

I held my breath. "She's beautiful, don't you think?"

"How do you know it's a she?"

Trust Mallory to dispute the gender. "I don't. It just seemed like a she to me." I grabbed Mallory's arm. "Isn't this incredible?"

The unicorn blinked. I gazed into its dark brown eye and a feeling of peace came over me.

"Mal, we're the only ones in our school who've ever been this close to a unicorn. Isn't that fantastic?"

Mesmerized by the creature, Mallory spoke, but her eyes

remained wide and her jaw slack. "But we won't be able to tell anyone. They'll think we're crazy." She stretched out her hand. "Do you think I can pet her?"

The unicorn gave a brief nod.

"I think she just gave you the go ahead."

Mallory slowly moved her hand toward the unicorn's muzzle and gently stroked its nose.

I couldn't help myself. I had to touch it too. For the briefest moment, I felt prickles on a bed of velvet.

At my touch, the unicorn dissolved into the air like a wisp of smoke. I turned toward Mallory, my eyes huge, and a laugh bubbling up. I grabbed her and we hugged each other, jumping up and down, shrieking with delight.

"That was awesome." I didn't care if we couldn't tell anyone. My best friend experienced a unicorn with me. We'd carry the memory for the rest of our lives.

When we reached the place where we left our stuff, I picked up the journal. "So what do you think now?"

"Definitely magic. Nothing else could have put a unicorn on our track. The odds against it are astronomical."

Since it truly had magic ... I picked up my pen and scribbled.

I will now be able to fly around the athletic field.

I dropped the journal on my backpack and waited.

Mallory's eyes grew big. "What did you write?"

A buoyancy filled me along with a desire to spring into the air. I bent my knees and jumped.

Mallory screamed as I zoomed up, up, up. I leaned forward and flew out toward the track. Amazing. I felt so free ... it was incredible.

The rushing wind became a jet stream behind me. I put my arms out to the side to better guide my flight. I couldn't believe it ... I was *flying!* A laugh bubbled up. This was by far, the coolest thing I had ever done in my life.

I glanced down at Mallory waving her arms like they were semaphore flags and jumping up and down. I should probably fly back to her and land. Besides, I had a ton more things I wanted to do with the journal.

As I approached the ground, I pulled back and slowed so when I hit the volleyball court I only had to run a few steps before I stopped.

I turned to face Mallory. "That. Was. *Awesome.*" In a few short strides I covered the ground back to my bag and scooped up the journal. "Do you want a turn?"

"No. What if someone had seen you? How would you explain flying around the school?"

What? Who cared?

Mallory tilted her head to the side. "Angela, think about it ... if anyone else in the school gets a whiff that you have a magic journal, *everyone* is going to want you to write something for them. And I don't think conjuring up a mountain of candy or making kids invisible counts as using the journal wisely."

She had a point. I'd get exhausted taking requests. And what if kids wanted stupid things and wasted the pages ... the journal wasn't all that long.

She tucked a stray piece of hair behind her ear. "Besides, we need time to examine how the journal works and possible repercussions. We need to keep it a secret."

"Okay." She was right we needed more time to figure out how it worked and how much it *could* do. I grabbed my pen. We needed time to study the book away from school.

I grinned. "I know ... I'll just write that school's out for the summer and—"

"Angela, no!" Mallory lunged toward me and wrestled the pen out of my hand. "Are you crazy? What if the magic wears off? How will I get into the Ivy League if I'm missing a year of middle school on my transcripts?"

Wow. I had always known Mallory took school seriously, but I didn't know she was already thinking about college. And Ivy League? Ambitious didn't quite cover it.

"Okay, Mal. I promise not to cancel school." Though for most kids, I'd be a hero for doing so. "We'd better eat before we have to go to class." I took my pen back and sighed.

A troublesome thought hit me as Mallory sat on the ground to finish her lunch. "Mal? What if my mom's job disappears like the gnome and the unicorn?"

Mallory chewed on her turkey sandwich and squinted at the sunshine. "I don't think it will."

I plopped down next to her. "Why not?"

She swallowed. "Well, for one thing, the company your mom got the job with is real, and she applied before you got your journal. But the unicorn and the gnome defy reality, so I don't think they could stay for long."

I hoped she was right. Another thought hit. One I couldn't stop giggling over. I grabbed the journal and scribbled quickly. And waited.

A fairy dressed in a lilac and purple dress, with short dark hair and rainbow wings stood next to Mallory and picked through the baggies of food. Mallory didn't notice.

And I wasn't going to tell her. I waited.

The cat, nose to the ground, hind end held high, crawled out of the bushes. One stealthy step at a time, it stalked the fairy as she checked out Mallory's lunch. I held back a snicker.

Mallory's nose wrinkled. "What is that obnoxious smell? Angela, did you fart?"

I broke out laughing. "No."

But then the smell reached me and my laugh turned to a cough. Mallory was right. Definitely foul.

"Then what is that smell? It's horrid." Mallory plugged her nose and her eye lit on the fairy. "What did you do, Angela?"

I took a deep breath to try to get my laughter under control. I nearly choked, which stopped the laughing.

"You're always saying fairy farts, so I thought I'd give you real ones."

I doubled over laughing at the look of outrage on Mallory's

face.

She got to her feet and backed away from the fairy. "Hey fairy, do you think you can keep your toots to yourself?"

The cat dodged Mallory to keep from getting stepped on. Before it could pounce on its target, the fairy drew herself up to her full height and flew into Mallory's face.

"I do not appreciate being called fairy. Do you like it when someone calls you girl?" She hovered with arms crossed, waiting for a response.

"What's your name, then?"

"Tatiana. And what may I call you?" Her arms dropped slightly.

"My name is Mallory and this is my friend, Angela." Her lip curled in disgust.

Tatiana must have let another fart fly. The cat dashed over and sat next to my backpack, twitching its tale, but stayed aloof.

"How does something so small put out such a powerful, evil smell?" She pinched her nose again.

"I have no idea what you are talking about." Tatiana's cheeks turned pink.

Mallory took a few steps toward me to get away from the smell. "I thought fairy farts were supposed to smell like roses."

I laughed so hard my side hurt and tears rolled down my cheeks. No matter where Mallory went, Tatiana followed.

"Angela, make her go away."

I tried to catch my breath.

Tatiana yelped. "Mallory, I think that is very rude of you.

I'm trying to make friends and you keep running away from me." Her squeaky little voice sounded indignant.

"Look Stinkerbell, I don't think this friendship is going to work. Maybe you can make friends with a skunk."

"Stinker ... Stinkerbell. Ha-ha-ha-ha-ha." I literally rolled on the ground laughing.

Mallory picked up the journal and dropped it on me. "Angela, I'm serious. Write in the book and make Tatiana disappear. She doesn't seem to be going the way of the gnome or unicorn."

Opening the journal, I quickly scrawled:

No more fairy farts.

We both stared at Tatiana, who flew to the grass, picked a dandelion and flew back. She didn't appear to be going anywhere.

"Um, what if I can't reverse it?" I tried to keep from giggling.

Mallory crossed her arms. "You'd better figure out a way."

Tatiana fluttered next to Mallory and plucked a petal off the dandelion. "She loves me ..." She pulled another petal off. "She loves me not ..." She let the petals flutter to the ground.

Mallory waved her hand in front of her nose. "Tatiana, dude. You've got to learn to control your flatulence."

Tatiana ignored her and continued plucking petals.

The five-minute warning bell rang.

Mallory clutched my arms. "Angela, what am I going to

do? Mr. Griffith won't understand Tatiana." Her eyes widened and her face paled. "What if we're the only ones who can see her and everyone thinks the obnoxious smell is coming from me? I'll die of embarrassment."

"Let me try again."

Tatiana will stop all flatulence and disappear.

Tatiana pulled the last petal off the dandelion and held it in the air. "She loves me." She flapped her colorful wings and flew up to Mallory's shoulder.

Mallory looked cute with a little lavender fairy sitting on her. Well, except for the stricken look of horror on her face.

Her shoulders slumped. "I'm going to have to get a gas mask and wear it for the rest of my life."

We gathered our stuff. "I don't know what to tell you. Maybe she'll disappear like the gnome and unicorn. The unicorn stayed a lot longer than the gnome. Maybe the journal is getting stronger."

As soon as I picked up my things, the cat rubbed up against my legs, but before I could pet it, it dashed back to the bushes.

"Where are we going, Mallory?" Tatiana zipped off and sped away.

Before we could take a step, she was back and threading flowers through Mallory's hair.

"Tatiana, I have to go to class. I can't wear flowers in my

hair. And I can't take a fairy to class with me."

Fluttering her wings, Tatiana crossed her arms and pouted. "But I want to stay with you."

Mallory searched the sky and took a deep breath. "But if you come with me to class, then the teachers will want to capture you and will keep you in a glass jar to study you." She held Tatiana in her palm. "You don't want to be examined, do you?"

She shook her head. "I think being kept in a jar would be horrible. They'd have to catch me first, though." She buzzed up into the sky, made a loop, and returned to Mallory's hand. Her body sagged. "Where should I wait for you?"

Mallory shot a look at me. I shrugged.

"I'll meet you back here after school, but we have to go or we'll get in trouble for being late." Mallory set her on a bush as we passed.

"I'll be waiting."

Tatiana hummed and used the branches of the bush as a trampoline.

We hurried away from the athletic field.

Mallory swung her pack to her shoulder. "Angela Ashby, have you saddled me with a farting fairy for life?"

Chapter Eleven - Bullies and Frogs

How I wound up taking history after lunch, when my brain wanted a nap, I'd never know. But today, wide awake with brain buzzing, I rehashed what happened with the journal instead of following the discussion about Pandora. I seesawed between awe over what the journal could do and amusement over Mallory and Tatiana.

The Tatiana incident showed me Madame Vadoma and Mallory were right; I needed to be careful about what I wrote in the journal, especially because it seemed nonreversible. Otherwise Tatiana would be gone, which would make me a little sad.

Once Mallory got over the whole noxious farting aspect, she might think it cool to have her own personal fairy. If Tatiana didn't disappear.

"Miss Ashby, will you please read the next paragraph."

Mr. Harris broke through my thoughts. I didn't even know what page we were on. I glanced at the open book next to me, and flipped a page. I opened my mouth to bluff my way through, but the bell rang. Phew.

Out in the hallway, Billy Shipman pinned Zach to the wall by the front of his shirt. Zach's feet weren't even touching the ground. Everyone gave them a wide berth. No one wanted to become Billy's next target. Clusters of students whispered to one another, and a few brave souls tried to inch past without attracting notice.

What had poor Zach done? Sometimes all it took was breathing in Billy's space.

Billy reminded me of a baboon I once saw at the zoo. He had small eyes, a long nose that ended in flared nostrils, and a vicious snarl.

I whipped the journal out of my pack. Here was a chance to use its magic for good.

> Billy Shipman is such a bully. He should get a taste of what it feels like to be bullied by someone bigger and stronger than him.

An angry yowling sound reached my ears as I quickly shoved the journal back in my pack so no one asked me about it. I scanned the hallway, but no one looked brave enough to have made the noise.

The outside doors flung open and all conversations stopped. I'd never seen the kid who came through the doors before. He wore biker boots, jeans, and a leather jacket with a

T-shirt underneath. His wallet was hooked to his studded belt with a chain. If Billy Shipman was big, this kid was humongous.

"Hey Shipman. What're you doing picking on a runt?"

Billy let go of Zach, who slid down the wall.

Once Zach's feet touched ground, he bolted.

The big kid reached Billy and shoved him in the chest. Billy slammed into the wall.

"Where were you?" He grabbed Billy by the shirt and hefted him in the air, just like Billy had done to Zach. "We got together and waited, but you were a no show."

Excited murmurs broke out from those who hadn't escaped the building.

"Do you see that …?"

"Finally, Billy's gettin' it."

"I—I c-c-can explain, Spike." The color left Billy's face.

Spike? What a name for the bully of the bully. It sounded like something you'd name your Pitbull.

Spike growled.

Maybe he *was* like a Pitbull gone bad.

His malice filled every crevice in the hallway. "No explanations. And no excuses."

He pulled Billy off the wall, raised him even higher, and slammed him against it again. Billy's head snapped back and banged the wall with a sickening *thunk*. Then Spike let go. Billy slid to the ground. He slumped against the wall, dazed.

A teacher poked his head outside the door. "Is there a problem here?"

Where had he been when Billy had Zach plastered against the wall?

Spike turned off his hostility, like someone flipped a switch, and the tension drained from the hall.

Billy shook his head and scrambled to his feet. "No problem. I tripped and fell."

The teacher stared at Billy and Spike for a few moments, hands on hips. Then he turned, muttering the whole way, and went back into his room.

As soon as the door closed, Spike's anger flared again. His voice quiet, he leaned in. "We're not through, Billy-boy. I'll see you at home." The puffs of his breath caused Billy's hair to jump with each word.

Spike was Billy's brother?

Then Spike walked forward, his shoulder slamming Billy into the wall one last time. The sound of his boots rang out as he left the building.

Everyone froze. No one wanted to move and catch Billy's attention. He might pick on someone just to show he was still in charge, not Spike. But no one looked away from him. It was like watching a wreck at the side of the road; not wanting to see the gore, but not being able to look away.

Billy surveyed the room and his face crumpled. "Quit staring at me." He bolted toward the door, unshed tears tightening his voice.

Whoa. Not something I thought I'd ever see. I touched the journal in my bag. Powerful stuff.

I held my breath before opening the door for Science. I liked Mr. Delgado, but hated walking into his class each day. The smell coming from the jars of frogs swimming in formaldehyde made my stomach turn. If I had to describe it, I think I'd say it smelled like all of nature died. Or maybe it smelled like rotting zombie farts.

I took my seat and breathed through my mouth until my nose acclimated to the stench. If the smell filled the room when the lids were on tight, I shuddered to think how it would smell when we opened them and had to dissect the frogs.

My stomach rolled.

Even fairy farts smelled better than formaldehyde.

The room was divided in half with the desks closest to the hallway door and the lab tables in rows against the outside wall. A frog nose pressed against the glass jar on the lab table closest to me. Shudders ran up my spine. I didn't want to dissect anything.

I wondered what it would take to get Mom to write a note saying dissection was against our religion. The school couldn't make me do anything against religious beliefs, could they?

Mom would never write such a note, so I'd probably embarrass myself by throwing up or passing out as soon as I cut into the frog. Someone made perfectly good computerized programs on dissection, why couldn't we use those instead of actual frogs?

Real frog dissection was a carryover from medieval times. No doubt it was a means of torture. *You defied the King? It's frog dissection for you!*

I glanced at Mallory's empty seat. She'd be the only reason I made it through this class.

Mallory couldn't wait until Mr. Delgado started the chapters on dissection. She thought the digital dissection lacked reality. Although, she thought it would be good practice for the real thing.

Mr. Delgado breezed into the room. Dressed in a collared shirt and tie, with creased slacks, he wore his thick and wavy dark hair brushed back from his forehead, except one stubborn curl that fell forward when he moved a lot. His goatee framed his mouth, and his teeth gleamed when he smiled. His dark eyes crinkled slightly at the edges when he laughed and his cologne carried a hint of spice.

His cologne completely made up for the formaldehyde stench.

Mallory scurried into the room and dropped her books on the desk with a thud. I swore her stack of books got larger every day. Soon she'd be hunchbacked from carrying them around.

Mr. Delgado quickly called roll and used his hook to pull down a frog chart from the ceiling.

He picked up his pointer stick from the dry erase board tray and tapped the chart. "Today we're going to learn how to make a frog sandwich."

Ew. I pictured the frog in the jar between two pieces of bread with the rubbery legs sticking out the side. Even with mustard to mask it, gross.

Mr. Delgado looked me straight in the eyes and grinned. "I know exactly what you're thinking." He made his voice squeaky. "Ew, Mr. Delgado. That's gross."

My face flushed.

"Let me explain what I mean. First we're going to start by reviewing the outer portion of the frog, or looking at the dorsal view."

He pulled down another chart. "Next we'll talk about the skeleton then the brain and nervous system, and so on."

He put the frog skeleton chart back up. "Once we learn all the parts of the frog, we'll know what we're looking at when we dissect them." He tapped the dorsal view chart with the pointer again. "Now let's get started."

Chairs scraped on the floor and papers rustled as everyone in the class got ready to take notes. I pulled out my notebook then grabbed the journal and sandwiched it between the pages.

"We'll start with an easy one." He slapped the pointer on the back leg of the frog picture. "Who can tell me what this is?"

Mallory's hand shot into the air.

Mr. Delgado scanned the room. "Trey. What is it?"

Trey slid sideways in his chair and his tongue flicked his upper lip. "The back leg, Mr. Del." He smirked at his buddies.

"And that answer will be wrong on the test."

Half the hands in the air dropped.

"What?" Trey sat straight in his seat.

Mr. Delgado pointed to the back of the class. "Zach, can you tell us?"

"Hind limb?" Zach's voice trailed up as if he wasn't one-hundred percent certain.

Trey chuckled.

"You are correct." Mr. Delgado clapped his hands together.

The smile left Trey's face and he grumbled.

Mr. Delgado rested the pointer on the ground. "Do you have a problem with the answer, Trey?"

"Yeah. In fancy restaurants they serve frog legs, not hind limbs."

Mr. Delgado rotated the stick between his palms. "Yes, you are correct. So if you're in a restaurant, you can call them legs, but here in my science class, they are limbs or they are wrong. Most times you don't order food in a restaurant by its scientific name." He tapped the frog's front limb. "Any guesses on what this is?"

Mallory's hand remained high in the air, intent on catching Mr. Delgado's attention.

I slipped the journal out from behind the pages so it looked like a part of the notebook while Sofia Pèrez answered the question. I propped my head on my hand to read the entries and wondered how the journal worked.

The frog in the jar stared at me. Creepy.

I felt Mr. Delgado's eyes on me. I needed to look like I was taking notes.

I don't want to dissect frogs. I think
it would be wonderful if the jar lids
disappeared, and the formaldehyde
turned to water, to stop the stink.
And the frogs came to life. Then
they could hop out of the jar and
escape to the great outdoors and
find a pond to live in.

"Who can tell me where the tympanic membrane is and what its function is?"

I glanced around the room. Everyone except Mallory dropped their hand. I thought the question should be *Who wants to know?* I faced front as Mr. Delgado called on Mallory.

The frog in the jar blinked at me.

Oh no. It took about a second and a half for the monstrosity of what had just happened to hit me. I had scribbled my fake notes in the *journal.* If I had written them in the notebook, nothing would be happening, except I'd be getting one class session closer to dissecting frogs.

But no, I had to screw up and write in the wrong book. Several frogs blinked and others flexed their fingers. I couldn't catch my breath. *Good grief … what had I done?*

My eyes widened when the jar lids disappeared. I sniffed. The air smelled fresher. Had my nose desensitized to the stench?

The window nearest the lab tables was cracked open.

Mr. Delgado called on Mallory.

The frog gripped the top of the jar with his long, webbed fingers.

"The tympanic membrane is on the side of the head behind the eye, and its function is hearing."

I heard Mallory answer the question, but the words sounded like gibberish as my heart beat rapidly and palms moistened while watching the frog pull up to the top of the jar. With his hind limbs, the frog gave a huge kick and landed on the table with a splat.

Sofia Pèrez jumped to her feet and screamed. More frogs hopped out.

Startled by her scream, Mr. Delgado rushed to Sofia. He had no idea what was wrong until a frog croaked. His head snapped back in surprise.

One frog kicked so hard to get out he knocked the jar over. Water spilled everywhere and the jar rolled slowly to the edge of the table.

Crash.

The glass smashed as it hit the floor and shards flew everywhere.

Screams filled the air along with chairs and desks scraping on the floor as kids jumped to their feet. Frogs hopped across the lab tables with a squishy sound and the occasional *ribbit* and headed toward the window.

Mallory's eyes looked like they would pop out and her jaw

dropped. "Did you …?"

The first frog made it to the window ledge and with a mighty leap and jumped out the window, taking the screen with it to the ground. More kids screamed and some ran to the furthest corner of the room.

Like an itty bitty frog would hurt them.

The rest of the class seemed frozen in time. Afraid to move; maybe even afraid to breathe.

Mr. Delgado tried to regain control. "Quiet!" He held both arms in the air.

All the screams and chatter stopped. The thump-squish of frogs hopping toward freedom took the edge off the quiet. A mass exodus of no-longer-to-be-dissected frogs.

A lock of Mr. Delgado's hair fell forward into his eyes. He whipped it back with his hand. "Class will now take place in the library. Please read the material about frog parts."

He surveyed the wreckage of his classroom. "How?"

Mallory grabbed my arm and pulled me toward the door. Hard.

As the rest of the class filed toward the outside doors, Mallory led me to the back.

She finally released my arm. "Angela Ashby, what did you do?"

"I didn't mean to." Well, not entirely. "It was an accident."

"How could dead frogs coming back to life and making an escape be an accident?" Scorn dripped from her words.

"Because I thought I wrote those things in my notebook,

but it was the journal." I did forget, sort of. But I couldn't feel bad about reanimating the frogs. They had a second chance at life, and I didn't have to cut them open. Win-win in my book.

Mallory covered her face with her hands and took a deep breath. When she finally dropped her arms, she pinned me with a glare. "You need to be careful about what you write in the journal, Angela. How is Mr. Delgado going to explain the frog resurrection? It's not like it will be a secret."

Oh, I didn't think about that. How would he explain the obvious dead hopping away? I'm surprised someone didn't start screaming about killer zombie frogs.

Mr. Delgado came to the door and put his hands on his hips. "You girls are supposed to be in the library."

"Yes, Mr. Delgado."

We hurried out of the building.

Chapter Twelve - After School

At the end of school, Mallory and I went back to the athletic field. Tatiana flitted around the bushes like a hummingbird. We stopped and watched her. Amazing. Seeing a fairy zipping around school made my brain feel like it had skipped a gear. I couldn't believe she was still here.

Why hadn't she disappeared? Did it mean fairies really exist?

When she spied us, she zoomed straight to Mallory.

"You came back." She sighed. "I'm so happy."

Mallory blushed. "I told you I'd be back."

"I thought you lied so you could ditch me." She shook her finger in Mallory's face. "I expected to have to hunt you down."

Mallory held her hand out, palm up, for Tatiana to land on. "I keep my promises."

"You should have been here earlier, Mallory. A frog pilgrimage passed by."

Mallory shot me a frown, her eyes glaring at me over the top of her specs. What did she expect me to do? She knew I couldn't reverse what had been written in the journal because Tatiana was still here.

Tatiana sank to a sitting position. "I tried to find out where they were headed, but they wouldn't stop. Poor things looked dry, so I gave them a little rain cloud for their travels."

What a weird and eerie sight it must have been—a trail of previously dead frogs hopping along with a low-flying cloud raining on them. It's a good thing no one had wandered out on the athletic field during class.

"Then a black cat jumped out of the bushes and tried to pounce on the frogs, but I turned the rain cloud into a thunder cloud and shot lightning at it." Tatiana's squeaky voice sounded indignant. "The cat dove back into the bushes after it hissed at me."

"Um, sorry we missed it." Mallory crossed her legs and sank to the ground in a fluid motion, causing Tatiana's wings to flutter. "I've been reading about malachite and its properties. It's very interesting."

When had she had time since this morning to do more reading about her crystal?

She rolled her eyes. "Don't look at me like that … I looked it up when we were in the library after you set the frogs free."

I sank down next to her. Typical. Mallory couldn't stand not to know something. So when the rest of us were pretending to read about frogs, she looked up crystals instead.

"You let the frogs go, Angela? You're the best." Tatiana practically swooned.

Mallory sighed. "Anyway, malachite has been used for thousands of years for healing, protection, drawing out negative emotions, and clarifying intention." She ticked the uses off on her fingers. "I'm sure that's why Madame Vadoma gave it to me."

"What's why?" I didn't see how that explained anything.

"She gave you the journal for a reason. I'm not sure what that is yet, but she must have known you'd need some help, especially with intention." She settled her glasses firmly on her nose. "Like with the frogs … It's also supposed to help with shyness and timidity."

If it could cure Mallory of being timid it would be quite some stone.

Some kids passed by the opening to the field and Mallory quickly lowered her hand into her lap to hide Tatiana from the passersby.

"Wheeeee!" Tatiana stood and crawled onto Mallory's leg. "That was fun."

Mallory glanced over her should to make sure no one paid any attention to us. "Do you know whether we're the only ones who can see you?"

Tatiana's laughter sounded like wind chimes tinkling. "Of course not, silly. Most people think I'm an exotic bird. They can't wrap their minds around seeing a fairy."

Seeing a fairy did take a little getting used to.

Mallory held her hand out. "Hop on." Then she unzipped her backpack and moved the hand with Tatiana toward the opening. "Climb in. I don't want anyone to recognize you as a fairy, and it will look strange if I have an exotic bird following me home."

Tatiana stiffened and flew off Mallory's hand. "But I'm afraid of the dark." Her voice rose even higher. "And I don't like being put in enclosed places."

Mallory grimaced and waved her hand in front of her face, then climbed to her feet. "Okay, calm down. I need a way to get you home with me safely."

Astonished, I stared at Mallory. I thought Tatiana irritated her, especially since she'd let off another stink-bomb.

"Hmmm." Tatiana tapped her finger against her cheek. "I know. I'll hide under your hair and sit on your shoulder." She ran up Mallory's arm and dived into her hair. "Can you see me, Angela?"

Mallory spun in a slow circle for me.

"Pull your wings in, Tatiana."

The wings folded and slipped into the hair.

"Okay, you're hidden." Good thing Mallory had thick long hair.

Mallory giggled. "Quit moving your wings. They tickle." She scooped up her pack. "Let's go."

Mom's car was in the driveway when I reached home. Despite Mallory's assurances that everything would be okay with Mom's new job, I hesitated on the porch before grabbing the door handle. Would I walk in to find her crying again?

Taking a deep breath, I clicked the latch and opened the door a crack. The smell of fresh baked cookies overwhelmed me.

Relief. Happiness sent Mom into the kitchen to bake. If anything bad happened with the new job, she wouldn't be baking.

I swung the door all the way open. "Mom, I'm home."

"Just in time, Angela. I took the cookies out of the oven two minutes ago." Her voice lilted with delight. "Your favorite—chocolate-chocolate chip. Hurry and put your things away."

I rushed to my room, dropped my bag on the bed, and flew back down the stairs.

Nothing beat warm cookies and ice-cold milk as an after-school treat.

I took a bite and enjoyed the slight crunch of the cooling cookie followed by the liquid chocolate of the melted chips. Mom hadn't baked in a long time.

She put a cookie on a napkin, grabbed her coffee, and joined me at the table. "How was your day?"

"Never mind my day." I would never be able to explain my day in a million years. "What happened with your job?"

She grinned. "I met my new boss first. She's wonderful."

Her coffee aroma mingled with the sweet scent of the cookie.

"She showed me around the office and told me my hours

would be flexible. And I'd be able to work from home, but will come into the office as needed."

Work from home? A smile spread across my face.

"I thought you'd like that. I'll have to go into the office for the first two weeks though." She raised the cup to her lips and gently blew.

"Then I went to Human Resources and they explained the benefits and gave me the salary information." She beamed. "I'll be making about a third more than before and the benefits are much, much better."

Bubbles of joy rose in me. "Fantastic, Mom. I'm so happy for you."

She broke off a piece of cookie. "Now, tell me about your day."

I stared at Mom's thimble collection on the wall and my mind scrambled for something to talk about. I couldn't start babbling about gnomes, unicorns, and farting fairies, not to mention a reanimated dead frog parade complete with low-flying rain cloud.

She'd think I'd lost my mind.

"Um, Cynthia tried picking on me today before school. With no one else around, she thought she could intimidate me."

Mom raised her eyebrows. "Have you tried being nice to her? She's probably jealous of your friendship with Mallory and wants to be friends."

I rolled my eyes. "She sure has a strange way of showing it. How can I be nice when she calls me names all the time?" Mom didn't understand how nasty Cynthia could be. "She starts it."

"But you don't have to finish it. Try making her your friend, Angela."

Why would I want such a horrible person as my friend? I needed to change the subject. My eyes stopped on the pewter thimble with the moose on top.

"Billy Shipman picked on Zach Taylor again today." Billy was like a bull moose compared to Zach. "But then a bigger boy than Billy came in and picked on him."

Oops. I shouldn't talk about Spike because I might slip and say something about the journal. "But a teacher came out and the other boy left."

Mom's forehead wrinkled in the middle like it always did when she was concerned. "Good. I don't like all the bullying going on at your school."

Who did? Well, except the bullies. Although, after today, I wasn't sure Billy Shipman thought so. And if Spike and Billy were brothers, maybe he got bullied more than I thought. I ate the last cookie and drained my milk.

"Thanks for the cookies, Mom."

Her face softened. "You're welcome, sweetie. I know it's been awhile, but things are going to be better from now on. I feel as if we've turned a corner."

I got up and hugged her. "I'm glad. You deserve some happiness for a change."

"Aw, thank you." She squeezed me tight. "You do too, you know." She patted my back and let go. "Your dad is going to take you out to dinner tomorrow night to make up for missing his time with you this weekend."

I froze. "I don't want to go."

She smoothed the bangs off my forehead. "He's making an effort. Give him a chance."

Yeah, right. "He's making the effort? Or you're making him?"

Mom must have badgered Dad about making things right. She always did. If he didn't want to see me without being hounded into it, then I didn't want to see him.

"He wants to explain to you what happened on Sunday. He feels bad about not picking you up."

I took a step back. "Because you guilted him into it."

Mom rubbed the crease between her brows like she had a headache. "I was angry with him on Sunday because he upset you. But once he explained, I understood. Give him the chance to explain it to you too."

"I guess I don't have a choice." I crossed my arms.

"Angela." Her tone turned sharp. "He's still your father."

"Not much of one. I never see him anymore."

"And he's trying to change that. Please Angela, just go to dinner and hear what he has to say."

Mom sounded exhausted. What happened to the happy bubbles she had when I got home? Had I argued them out of her?

"Fine. I'll go to dinner with him."

She gave me a weak smile.

My history homework wouldn't wait any longer. If I didn't get it finished, I'd fail. Mr. Harris didn't accept late assignments. If you didn't turn it in on the right day, he gave you a zero. I'd finished most of the reading, but hadn't answered the questions yet.

It wasn't fair. Pandora's story should have been English homework, not history. But the school combined history with social studies and decided the study of myths belonged in social studies. If we studied the myths in English, Mrs. Clark would make it interesting.

Pandora would walk out of the book and stroll through the classroom practicing her wiles. Prometheus would be in a huddle of kids dreaming up devilry.

Mr. Harris just barked out facts and expected you to remember them. He made Greek Gods boring. And now I had to answer questions.

At least the first question wasn't hard. *In what country does the story of Pandora take place?* Duh. It's *Greek* mythology. I scribbled my answer.

Who were Pandora's parents? Ha. Trick question. She didn't have any.

The corner of the journal showed in the backpack opening. I reached toward it.

Ping. A chat message from Mallory.

How R U? What R U doing?

I grabbed the keyboard.

Homework. Ugh.

Mallory's status changed to typing.

I promised T I'd show her how chat
worked.

T? T, who?

It took me a minute to figure out she meant Tatiana.

How is she doing?

Fine. Stinky. I'm going to have to
sleep with the window open.

The cursor blinked for a moment then Mallory began typing again.

I blame you and your journal, just so
you know.

I drummed my fingers briefly on the desk.

Speaking of the journal, I thought
about writing that my homework was
already finished. Just to see what
would happen.

As soon as I hit send, Mallory's status changed to typing.

You'd cheat?

Even though we were on chat, I heard Mallory's outrage in my head.

T told me she'd finish my homework
with some fairy dust, but I wouldn't
let her.

Trust Mallory to stand on the moral high ground.

But what if I wrote that no teachers

would assign homework for the rest
of the year?

Immediately after I hit send, my computer shut down.
What the heck happened? It was like someone had pulled the
plug out of the socket. But the cord was firmly plugged in at
both ends.

After checking over my shoulder to make sure I was still
alone in my room, I turned the machine back on and waited for
it to boot up. Freaky.

As soon as I was back online, I chatted Mallory.

I'm back.

The cursor blinked for a few moments.

I gotta go, but Angela, please don't
write about no homework.

I felt like Mallory wanted to say more, but didn't.

K. Better get back to it then.

See you tomorrow."

Mallory's status went to offline.

I glanced at the journal again. No homework for the rest
of the year was a brilliant idea. And several kids would thank
me, if they only knew. Of course, I couldn't tell them. Would it
really hurt?

Then Tatiana came to mind. I couldn't make her go away
when Mallory begged me to. And using the journal to get out of
homework might be stretching the whole, '*use it wisely*' thing.

Maybe I should just finish my homework.

Why did Zeus command Hephaistos to create Pandora? Mr.

Harris would probably blow a gasket if I put my real answer. *Zeus was a whiny crybaby who wanted everything to go his way.*

Mrs. Clark would let me answer that way, but she'd make me expand and tell her why Zeus whined.

With a sigh, I finished answering all the questions.

Then I pulled the journal out. It couldn't hurt to write my thoughts about what happened today, could it? It's not every day a girl sees a gnome, pets a unicorn, sets previously dead frogs on a pilgrimage, and conjures up a farting fairy. I chuckled. Even the memory of Mallory's face when she smelled the farts made me laugh.

And it might help me to write my feelings about dinner tomorrow night with Dad. Even though I agreed to go, I did it to make Mom happy, not because I wanted to.

I filled several pages before putting the journal aside and calling it a night.

Chapter Thirteen - Cynthia Lashes Out

I clumped down the stairs in the morning to find Mom pouring coffee. When she set the pot down, it clanked against the warming plate. She's lucky it didn't break.

"Morning, sweetie. Toaster waffles?" She pulled the box out of the freezer.

"Sure."

She plunked a couple in the toaster and pressed the lever. I grabbed a glass of orange juice and went out to the table.

Mom sipped her coffee in the kitchen. She stared off into space. Then a couple minutes later shook her head and took another sip of coffee.

I went back into the kitchen. No fragrance of waffles greeted me. I felt the toaster. Stone cold.

"Uh, Mom?" I held up the cord. "They'd probably toast faster if this was plugged in." I put the plug in the socket.

"I'm sorry. I didn't think."

I shrugged and leaned against the counter to wait. "No biggie. So what's wrong?"

Mom poured some more coffee and missed the cup. The hot, brown liquid splashed the side of the coffeemaker and ran down the counter and over the edge.

"Oh." I grabbed some paper towels and threw them on the floor where the coffee had pooled.

"How much sleep did you get last night?" I picked up the cup, topped it with coffee, and handed it to Mom. "You go sit at the table. I'll clean this up while my waffles cook."

"You didn't make the mess, so you shouldn't have to clean it up." Mom looked upset.

"Don't worry. Think of all the messes I've made. I owe you one or two." I grinned. "Or you can owe me. Just go sit down. I've got it."

I planted my hands in the middle of her back and gave her a push. It took me a couple minutes to clean up the mess and by that time my waffles were done.

"What's up with you this morning?" I plunked my plate on the table.

"I'm a little nervous about starting this new job. I'm afraid they won't like my work, or it will take me too long to get acclimated." She rubbed her forehead. "I know I'm being ridiculous, but this job means so much to me. I want everything to work out well."

"Just go and do your best and they'll love you." I slathered the waffle in butter and watched it melt.

"How did you get to be so smart?"

I winked. "I must take after my Mom."

"Do you mind if I take you to school a little early again today? I want to make sure I'm there without having to stress about traffic."

I shook my head. "I don't mind."

I waited for Mallory in my usual morning spot on the edge of the planter. The black cat marched along the ledge. It seemed to hang out at school a lot. Mallory trotted up the school's front steps. I waved. She grinned and headed in my direction.

She made it halfway when Cynthia burst out of the bathroom and cut her off.

"Have a nice trip, Mallory." She pushed Mallory in the back and stuck her foot in front of Mallory's ankle.

Tatiana swung out clutching a hunk of Mallory's hair. Her rainbow wings glinted in the early morning sun. Mallory lost her grip on her books and her glasses skittered across the concrete.

I jumped to my feet. I didn't know whether to help Mallory or punch Cynthia first. That was totally uncalled for.

But Mrs. Clark stormed toward Cynthia, who laughed at Mallory as she landed on the ground.

When Mallory hit the ground, Tatiana scrambled back under her hair and her wings disappeared from view. Hopefully no one noticed a fairy in a lavender dress swinging like Tarzan from Mallory's head.

Mrs. Clark pointed her finger in Cynthia's face. "You stay right here." Then she helped Mallory to her feet.

Her palms bled where the concrete had scratched them

"Are you all right, dear?" Mrs. Clark patted Mallory on the back.

I hoped Tatiana stayed securely against Mallory's neck. She'd be difficult to explain. Even to Mrs. Clark.

Mallory nodded.

"You." Mrs. Clark turned an angry face to Cynthia. "Pick up those books and apologize."

Mrs. Clark would take care of Cynthia, but I couldn't stand by and do nothing. Especially when she'd hurt Mallory and Tatiana could have been squished. I pulled the journal out.

Cynthia Benson is so mean. She deserves to have humongous warts erupt all over her big nose. And they should burn.

I slammed the journal shut and the cat hissed and arched its back, its eyes flashing. Then I picked up Mallory's glasses.

Cynthia concentrated on picking up all Mallory's books, which had scattered across the concrete spilling papers everywhere. After putting the English book in the bag, Cynthia rubbed her nose. She grabbed another book and rubbed her nose again.

I felt a chuckle forming in my stomach and tried to keep

the smile off my face. When Cynthia stood, the beginning of a wart grew smack on the end of her nose.

She finished picking up the books and shoved the bag in Mallory's trembling hands. "Sorry you're such a klutz." Mallory nearly fell over again.

"Young lady we have a date with Mr. Lassiter. Let's go." Mrs. Clark held her arm out toward the office.

Cynthia clutched her nose and howled. "My nose huuuurrrts."

Mrs. Clark took a step closer to her. "We'll check your nose *after* you see the vice principal. Tripping another student is unacceptable."

Cynthia's voice muffled as she tightly pinched her nose. "I'm not going anywhere with you."

Mrs. Clark closed the gap between them. "You have injured another student and ..."

"Back off." Cynthia shoved Mrs. Clark on the shoulders with both hands.

My eyes widened and I watched in horror as Mrs. Clark took a step back and tried to steady herself. But the heel of her shoe broke and she fell to the ground.

I ran to Mrs. Clark. Mallory and I helped her to her feet.

She reached out and grabbed Cynthia's shoulder. "We're going to see the vice principal. Now."

Mrs. Clark clumped off with an unsteady gait because she wore only one shoe, and pulled Cynthia with her. Then she kicked her shoe off, grabbing it as it spiraled through the air and didn't miss a step.

I didn't think I could admire her more than I already did. I was wrong.

Cynthia complained bitterly about her nose the entire way.

"Are you okay?" I picked up one of Mallory's homework papers Cynthia missed and handed it to her along with her glasses.

"My hands sting a bit, but they should be okay."

I lowered my voice. "And how about you, Tatiana?"

"You can call me T."

It seemed strange to hear her chirpy, little voice coming out from Mallory's hair. I mouthed 'T' at Mallory, who rolled her eyes. She'd tell me later.

Mallory's hair rustled as Tatiana paced. "Who is that battle-ax, Mallory? I think I need to mix her up a little potion."

Mallory took a deep breath and sighed. "No, Tatiana ... I mean T."

We walked toward the athletic field followed by the black cat. I didn't see it hanging out with any of the other kids, so it seemed to have adopted us.

After peering at her glasses, Mallory slid them into place. "Mrs. Clark will take care of Cynthia. She's gonna be in enough trouble without you making a potion. Remember, we talked about no magic."

I clutched Mallory's arm. "I can't believe T does magic and you're not letting her."

She pushed her glasses firmly back into place. "I think we need to be cautious with magic, and make sure we think through the consequences before using it."

She turned fierce eyes on me. "And we have enough magic with your journal. Just think what would have happened if the gnome and the unicorn hadn't disappeared on their own. At least T is small enough to hide and not half the size of an elephant."

She reached up to her shoulder and placed Tatiana on a bush. "And look what happened with your mom. The first thing you wrote cost her a job."

I choked down my guilt. "But I got a better one for her." Couldn't Mallory see the bright side of things?

"You were lucky you could." She narrowed her eyes. "What did you do to Cynthia's nose?"

I giggled. I couldn't help it. "I couldn't let her get away with hurting you, so I gave her humongous, burning warts."

Mallory's brow furrowed and her mouth opened in a big O. "Don't you understand you made things worse? Because of the warts, she pushed Mrs. Clark and made her fall."

I shrugged. "But she'll be in more trouble. Mrs. Clark looked okay. Well, except her shoe."

"But it shouldn't have happened."

"I wasn't going to stand by and let Cynthia bully you."

Tatiana flew up and perched on Mallory's head. "I'm with Angela on this one. We both could have been hurt. Someone needed to do something."

She flew to me and held her arm outstretched. "High five."

I tapped my index finger against her palm.

She giggled. "Oops. Excuse me. Fairy farts." She zoomed away.

I braced myself for the stench, but it didn't come. "What did you do? She doesn't stink so much today." I put my hands on my hips. "I thought you said no magic."

"I didn't use magic. I used an air sanitizer." Her eyes sparkled. "I drenched my dad's old handkerchief in it then cut it up and made a lining for T's dress."

Only Mallory would come up with a solution like air sanitizers.

"And T and I are working together to discover what is causing her flatulence problem. We're trying different foods and recording the results."

What a science geek. And one of the reasons she was my best friend. I loved how she knew there had to be an answer and wouldn't give up until she figured it out.

The bell rang and Tatiana sped back to us. I swear she had a sparkly trail behind her. "I'll wait here for you, M. You and A have fun in class."

As we walked toward the buildings, I nudged Mallory. "So what is with T and M and A?"

Mallory shrugged. "She thought it was funny when I called her T last night on chat because I didn't want to type her full name. And ever since, she's insisted upon T."

I laughed. "Fairies are funny. I'm glad you two are getting along."

"Yeah. Once I figured out how to destinkify her, things got a lot better. It is kinda cool being the only one around to have a fairy."

Chapter Fourteen - Unintended Consequences

I arrived in English to find a sub, Mr. Farber, standing at the front of the room. What if Mrs. Clark was more hurt than I thought? Would it be my fault?

Taking my seat, I watched as my classmates filed in the room. When they saw Mr. Farber, they whispered to their nearest neighbor, so it sounded like a room full of leaking beach balls.

The hissing stopped when Mr. Farber called the class to order. He and Mrs. Clark were complete opposites. While she dressed conservatively, usually wearing a suit each day, Mr. Farber looked like he just came in from the beach, with his baggy pants, docksides with no socks and collared Hawaiian print shirt worn open over a T-shirt. He even wore sunglasses on top of his head. But opposite to their dress, Mrs. Clark allowed us freedom, where it was rumored Mr. Farber had regulations for his rules.

Complete silence filled the room, except for the occasional creaking chair. Mr. Farber did a military style roll call, barking out each name and expecting an immediate response. With a last name of Ashby, I answered first then relaxed through the remainder.

The door screeched open and an office assistant walked up to Mr. Farber and handed him a note. He frowned at the interruption as he opened the folded paper.

"Angela Ashby."

My spine straightened and I caught my breath.

"Please take your things and go to the office."

Whispers and suppressed laughter rippled through the room.

"But I didn't do anything. Why do they want me?" My stomach clenched.

Mr. Farber gave the note back to the office girl. "It doesn't matter why. And the note didn't say. Please take your things and leave so we can continue the class without further interruption."

All eyes in the room were fixed on me as I picked up my books and shoved them in my backpack. How embarrassing. I couldn't get out the door fast enough. But once in the hall, my steps slowed. I dreaded reaching my destination.

The office girl walked ahead of me and turned back to make sure I still followed.

I did.

Slowly.

She stopped halfway across the quad. "They do want you there today, you know." She huffed and started off again.

My stomach knotted and with each step it lurched a little

more.

The door to the office clanged shut behind me with such finality, the only thing missing was the sign from *Dante's Inferno*.

Abandon all hope, ye who enter here.

I certainly felt like the hope had been sucked right out of me.

Mallory sat outside the principal's office, head down and dejected, she looked miserable.

As I approached, she raised her head and opened her mouth, but before she could say a word, the door to the office opened.

"Angela, please come in."

The office, though large, felt claustrophobic. Too many people inside. Mr. Lassiter and Mrs. Murphy, the principal, sat behind the desk and in front of the desk to the left was Cynthia and her parents and to the right, Mrs. Clark.

My stomach did another roll. This didn't seem to be a good thing at all. Mrs. Clark looked frightened, and Cynthia smirked. It should be the other way around.

Mr. Lassiter pointed to the only vacant chair. "Have a seat, Angela. We want to ask you a few questions."

I felt for the chair with my arm and edged into it, not taking my eyes off Mr. Lassiter.

Mrs. Murphy leaned forward. "There's no reason to be afraid, Angela. We need to ask you some questions about what happened this morning."

I nodded, my eyes widening.

"Now, this morning before school, did you see Mrs. Clark grab Cynthia?"

"Yes, but ..."

"Ha." Cynthia's dad rocked back on his heels and crossed his arms.

The smile on his face made him look like a shark getting ready to chomp its prey.

Cynthia's mom stared straight ahead. "My poor baby." Her tone was deadpan.

Did she even care? And Cynthia was no one's poor baby. She was a terror.

My heart sank. Mrs. Clark wouldn't look at me.

"Wait a minute." My voice rose in desperation to set the record straight. "Let me finish."

Mrs. Murphy folded her hands. "No need to worry, Angela. You've told us what we needed to know."

"No, I haven't." I stood, knocking the chair back. "You didn't ask the right question. You should have asked me why."

Unfallen tears choked me for a moment. "You didn't ask me about what happened to Mallory. How Cynthia tripped her for no reason." My indignation rose. "On purpose."

I swallowed to clear my throat. "And Mrs. Clark came to help Mallory and Cynthia pushed her. She fell, ruining her shoe. Then, because Cynthia refused to come to the office, she took her by the shoulder."

I glanced at Mrs. Clark. A glint appeared in her eye and the ghost of a smile crossed her lips.

"What was she supposed to do? Allow Cynthia to beat up Mallory and attack a teacher because she didn't want to go to the office?"

Mr. Lassiter held his hands up. "Now Angela, calm down."

"How can I calm down when you're trying to ..." What was the word Mrs. Clark had taught us that meant forcing someone to do something they didn't want to? *Oh, yeah.* "... to *railroad* Mrs. Clark into admitting she did something wrong by protecting Mallory?"

Mr. Lassiter rose from his chair, but Mrs. Murphy tapped her pencil on the desk and he sank down again.

She fixed me with her gaze. "Angela, we're not trying to railroad anyone. We are gathering the facts so we can properly assess the situation." Her voice took on a soothing tone. "Thank you for sharing your information with us. Now, please take a seat outside the office, in case we have more questions for you."

Dismissed.

As I left, I glanced at Cynthia. Even the sight of the three huge warts on her nose didn't bring me any joy. At least she didn't look as confident as when I walked in.

She glowered at me and mouthed the words '*I'll get you.*'

Did she think no one else saw her mouth moving? I glanced around the room before walking out. Maybe she had a point—no one paid any attention to us.

I slumped into the chair next to Mallory and dropped my backpack on the ground.

Mallory stared at her feet. "I feel awful. They wouldn't let me say anything about Cynthia starting it."

I patted her shoulder. "They tried to do the same thing to me, but I told them anyway."

"Now do you understand what you caused by giving Cynthia warts? Mrs. Clark could lose her job."

I pulled my hand from her shoulder. "You're blaming me?"

The secretary looked in our direction. Oops. I forgot where we were.

I lowered my voice and hissed. "Cynthia's the one who pushed her."

"You need to remember, Angela ... 'With great power comes great responsibility.'"

"Spiderman?" I couldn't believe Mallory had quoted from a comic book.

She gave me a withering stare. "Voltaire."

The door opened and Mrs. Murphy poked her head out. "Mallory? Please join us again."

Mallory jumped in her seat and popped up. She walked stiff-legged into the office as if she were on her way to face a firing squad.

The door barely closed before I pulled out my journal. I needed to do damage control. I couldn't undo Cynthia's warts or her reaction to them, but I might be able to help influence things in Mrs. Clark's favor. She didn't deserve to be in trouble for helping Mallory.

Please let all the adults understand Mrs. Clark was doing her job. She protected Mallory from being bullied and didn't do anything wrong. She needs the school to understand and support her. Cynthia was out of control and had to be stopped.

I stopped writing. A small voice inside me asked the question I didn't want to know the answer to. *Did Cynthia rampage out of control because of what I had done?*

I stared at the words and tried to think of ways they might go wrong, because everything else I wrote in the journal seemed to. Except the gnome and unicorn, and they disappeared. I hoped my words would be enough to counteract the damage already done. I closed the journal and shoved it back in my pack.

The door opened and Mallory came out and sat next to me again.

"Well?"

She took her glasses off and polished them. "They let me talk this time and asked me more about what happened with Cynthia." She put her glasses back on. "Now they're going to contact my mom and have her come down to discuss the incident." Mallory glared at me. "I didn't want my mom to know I was being bullied. She'll think I can't handle it."

I understood her anger. Nobody liked to be called a victim.

"I'm really sorry, Mal. But maybe this is for the best because they'll make Cynthia stop."

Scorn curled the edge of her lips. "Do you honestly believe Cynthia will stop picking on people?" She gave a short, bitter laugh. "She'll make sure she's not seen. But it's not going to stop."

"You don't believe people can change?"

"I believe people can change, but I don't believe she will. She enjoys her meanness too much." She buried her face in her hand. "This is a nightmare."

I tapped my fingers against my thigh. "It'll get better. The school's taking care of it."

"Yeah, right. I feel like they've put a target on my back and announced—*this one here can be bullied, so take your shots now.*"

I didn't know what to say. I collapsed against the chair. In a way she was right. If the school made a big production about protecting her, they might as well have tossed her into a piranha tank.

Mallory grabbed my wrist. "Angela, you've got to stop writing in that journal. Please." She rarely asked me for anything and this time she pleaded.

"But Mal ..."

The door opened again and Mrs. Murphy stepped out. "Angela, thank you so much for your input. You may return to class now."

Mallory looked up with hope gleaming in her eyes.

"We'd like you to wait, Mallory. We've contacted your mother and she should be here soon." Mrs. Murphy went back into her office as Mallory slumped in her chair.

She cupped her hands around her mouth and put them to my ear as she whispered. "If my mom makes me go home, don't forget T. Bring her to me after school."

I put my hand on her shoulder. "I think you'll be here to carry her home yourself, but if not, I'll remember T."

I glanced at the clock as I walked out of the office. The bell for lunch would ring in fifteen minutes. I wasn't going back to class to have Mr. Farber yell at me for disrupting it again. I headed toward the library. I needed to think.

Chapter Fifteen - Mallory Pushes Back

My footsteps clumped as I trudged across campus to the library. Mallory had never been this upset with me before. She blamed me for everything and it wasn't fair. Cynthia was the one who started it.

When I reached the library door, the black cat wound itself around my legs, then followed me in. Though I doubted cats were allowed in the library, no one said anything as it trotted beside me, tail held high. I went to the reading corner at the back and flopped into the big stuffed chair. I buried my face in my hands and closed my eyes while the cat rubbed its head against my legs.

The memory of Mrs. Clark's fear flashed in my head. My eyes flew open and I stared through my fingers.

Mrs. Clark, who always handled everything without turning a hair. How could she be afraid?

Was Mallory right? Was I responsible?

Or would Cynthia have pushed Mrs. Clark anyway?

Did the warts on her nose have nothing to do with it? Or

was I hoping they didn't so I wouldn't feel guilty?

I pulled out the journal and opened it to the last entry. Pen poised over the page, I hesitated. The cat jumped into my lap and I stroked its fur. I didn't know what else to write. Inflicting some sort of pain on Cynthia sounded like a good idea. I wanted her to suffer.

The cat gave a low-pitched growl.

But what if it backfired, like the warts? "What do you think, cat? Bad idea?"

It gazed directly into my eyes and blinked.

"Yeah, you're probably right." I recapped the pen and put it away.

Good grief. Now I was taking advice from a cat. I should probably name the cat, since it seemed to have adopted me. Maybe it was like Mallory's crystal and helping me with intention. It stopped me from writing something more to hurt Cynthia. So I should name it for the rock.

I scratched the cat under the chin. "I think I'll call you Malachite. What do you think?"

It purred and blinked at me with those big amber eyes again.

"I'm going to take that as a yes, so Malachite it is. But I'm going to have to go because the lunch bell will ring soon."

As I closed the journal, a thought struck me. I had written on several pages, and because the journal was thin, I should have filled it already. I counted the blank pages. The number of clean, blank pages in the book remained the same. Did the journal grow with use? I opened it again to inspect it.

Flipping through my entries, I saw they were all there. Between chronicling my days and using the journal to make things happen, I filled twenty-three pages. But I still had twenty-five blank ones. Closed, the journal remained the same width. How could the number of pages have doubled but not the thickness?

I wanted to show Mallory, but didn't know whether she'd even talk to me anymore. Maybe during lunch she'd let me show her. If she forgave me for her mom being called in.

That part was so unfair. I wasn't to blame.

Warts or no warts, Mrs. Clark would have taken Cynthia to the vice principal's office and Mr. Lassiter would have called Mallory's mom to come down to discuss the bullying. The school anti-bullying policy included calling the parents of both the bully and the victim.

I had first-hand experience with the policy because just after Cynthia moved in she tried to blame me for bullying her. It was all a big mistake, but when the school told me they had called Mom, I shook until she arrived.

Cynthia had been playing hopscotch all by herself and she tripped and fell when she'd tried to jump the first three squares. I ran over to help her because she was crying. She pushed my hand away when I'd tried to help her up. When she stood I'd rubbed her back, like Mom would do when I was hurt, and said something stupid like *You'll be all right.'*

Cynthia shrieked *'she's hurting me'* over and over and when the teacher came to see what had happened, she lied and said I'd pushed her.

Since then we'd never gotten along. Before that Cynthia never played with anyone and wouldn't even talk unless answering a question. Afterward it was like because of what'd happened she figured out she could intimidate other kids—and Mallory and I became her favorite targets. It was weird because I'd only wanted to help, but a bully was born.

The school thought they'd solved a problem, but until they changed how things were handled, bullies would keep bullying.

I'd need to be on the alert to help protect Mallory. Too bad she wouldn't let Tatiana use magic. I'd love to see what a little fairy could do to a big bully. And Tatiana would love to get back at Cynthia for tripping Mallory.

It was funny, but since the moment Tatiana appeared, she and Mallory belonged together. She talked to me, but all her attention focused on Mallory. Maybe I should wish for my own fairy.

I opened the journal again and Malachite put a paw on the page, right under my last entry. Almost as if it were pointing to it. *Get a grip, Angela. Cats don't point.* I gazed into its amber eyes. It was a cat, behaving like a cat, and nothing more.

I reread my last entry and the last words I had written mocked me.

How could I ask for something as frivolous as a fairy when I had put Mrs. Clark's teaching career in jeopardy? I couldn't. Besides, I had a part time cat, and Malachite would probably think a fairy was nothing more than a good snack.

Snapping the cover closed, I put Malachite on the ground, snatched up my bag, and stormed out the door. Thinking about things made me feel worse.

Having a journal that gave you what you asked for should have been the best thing in the world. Life should be fabulous and full of flying and pizza deliveries to class. Instead, I felt like everything was going wrong.

I waited at the lunch tables to see whether Mallory would join me. The wind carried the lunch smells from the cafeteria. The scent of tacos and corn dogs battled with mustard and pickles from the homemade lunches.

Odd. I would have expected Malachite to have followed me to the lunch area so it could beg for handouts. But as soon as we left the library, it disappeared.

Exiting the building across the quad, Billy Shipman pushed past the other kids. Shoving, flicking ears, and body slamming, he was worse than ever. The more I watched him the angrier I got. He should have learned something when Spike terrorized him.

Obviously not.

He approached the planter as dark clouds rolled in casting shadows over the entire quad.

I whipped out the journal and wrote:

> Billy should run into the planter and
> trip over it.

That'd show him. He should pay attention to where he walked instead of plotting who to hurt next.

Lightning flashed and the sky crackled.

"Bwauck ... bwauck." He walked next to Zach and flapped his arms. "How's Chicken-boy?" The thunder nearly drowned out Billy's taunts.

Zach barely glanced at Billy and quickened his step.

I shook my head. Zach was trying to do what the school taught about bullies—ignore them and walk away. Like Billy wouldn't be able to keep up. I held my breath. They had reached the planter.

Billy's foot caught the corner of the planter as he raised his hand to whack Zach on the back of the head. Both boys crashed to the ground and Billy landed on Zach.

Malachite leaped out from the shrubbery in the center of the planter and paced along the edge.

When Billy scrambled to his feet, he kicked Zach in the midsection. "Watch where you're going, Chicken-boy." He kicked Zach's book bag across the quad.

Zach lay on the ground, moaning. His ribs had to be cracked from the kick Billy gave him.

I spotted Ms. Landau a building over. She faced the other direction, but she had to have heard the commotion going on behind her. Why didn't she go help Zach? Was she afraid of getting into trouble like Mrs. Clark?

Billy Shipman didn't seem to care that a teacher was nearby.

The way rumors spread, everyone on campus knew what'd happened between Cynthia and Mrs. Clark by now. Soon it would be the stuff of Liberty Middle School legend. And the bullies would rule the school if the teachers were afraid to face them down.

Mallory ran up behind me. "What happened to Zach? Why isn't anyone helping him?"

She dropped her lunch on the table and ran to Zach. She stopped just short of where he lay and her back stiffened as she gazed at him. Then she knelt and held out her hand.

Billy towered over Mallory. "Leave the little worm alone."

My heart jumped into my throat. Was Mallory about to get pounded? I stood and my muscles tensed, ready to run to her rescue.

Mallory jumped to her feet and shoved her finger right in Billy's face. "You're nothing but a big coward, Billy Shipman."

Billy jerked his head away from her finger and stepped back.

Snickers ran through the gathering crowd. The sight of Billy Shipman recoiling from Mallory would delight many for quite some time.

But I feared the backlash. Running over, I elbowed my way through the crowd until I stood next to Zach.

"I am not a coward." Billy's face turned red and his nose wrinkled as he frowned and took a step forward. He leaned in, his fists tightened and the veins popped out on his neck. "You'd better watch what you say, runt."

Ms. Landau glanced our direction then turned away. Should I help Mallory, or go back and write something in the journal to calm the situation?

Mallory made a big production of yawning and patting her mouth. "Threats are getting old. Of course you can beat me up. You're bigger than me."

Amazed, I stared at Mallory.

"You're twice my size, for crying out loud."

She'd let Cynthia walk all over her, but now she laid down the law to Billy Shipman as if she'd been doing it her whole life. Maybe her crystal was more than just a pretty rock.

I held out a hand to help Zach up from the ground. He grunted as I pulled him by the arm and his body stayed hunched.

"Yeah. You need to leave us alone." He clutched his side where Billy had kicked him.

Billy sneered at Zach. "You looking to get beat up again, Taylor?" He shook his head. "You just don't learn, do you?"

I jumped between Zach and Billy.

Mallory planted a hand in the middle Billy's chest and stopped him from moving forward. "Do you think picking on Zach makes you look like a tough guy?"

Mallory? I couldn't believe my eyes.

She appealed to the crowd. "Does anyone think Billy is cool or tough for beating up Zach?"

Murmurs rippled through the mob. Someone at the back yelled *No!* More and more voices called out *No*, until they ran together.

Ms. Landau wouldn't be able to ignore things for much longer.

Billy spun and tried to see who spoke out so he could make threats, but there were too many.

Mallory turned and whispered to me. "Help me up."

She put her foot on the planter ledge and I let her use my shoulder to climb on top. She held up both hands to quiet the crowd.

Chapter Sixteen - Broken Friendship

Although shorter than most of her classmates, Mallory made an impressive figure standing with arms outstretched and fingers splayed, the sun glinting off her glasses. She stood statue still, rigid except her hair, which swirled in the breeze. No trembling knees or anything else.

The chatter slowed and an eerie quiet spread through the quad as everyone waited for Mallory to speak. She lowered her hands to her side.

"It's time to warn the bullies in this school. We're done!"

Not a stutter in sight.

Everyone in the quad stared at her, spellbound. Except Billy. His nose wrinkled and upper lip curled; he looked confused.

"We're done trying to avoid their notice. We're done being afraid some coward will pick on us. And most of all, we're done standing by and watching them pick on our friends."

The crowd's rumblings surged.

"If we stick up for one another, the bullies will back down.

Together, there are more of us than there are of them, and they can't take us all on at once."

Mallory scanned the eyes of the kids gathered round. "Who is with me?" Her arm shot back up in the air. "No-More-Bullies! No-More-Bullies!" She punctuated each word with a fist pump.

Zach and I joined her during the second time through, clapping with each word. "No-More-Bullies!"

One by one more voices joined the chant until the entire quad chanted and clapped with Mallory. Ms. Landau finally faced our direction.

While everyone focused on Mallory, I snuck a glance at Billy Shipman and nearly laughed. His face showed a mass of emotions. Surprise, frustration, anger … and the hint of fear. His fists clenched and unclenched as if he didn't know what to do. He must have finally realized being bigger than everyone else didn't work against so many.

He pushed Andrea as he tried to make his way out of the crowd. She pushed back. Billy cocked his fist.

And froze.

The kids in the group circled behind Andrea, still chanting but changed from clapping to slugging their palms.

Billy dropped his arm and fled.

The crowd erupted in cheers.

Ms. Landau made her way through the clumps of students. Andrea called out to her as she passed, and she stopped. From the look of things, the kids surrounding Andrea weren't wasting any time filling Ms. Landau in on what happened.

Zach held up his hand to help Mallory off the planter ledge, but doubled over in pain before he raised it halfway.

"C'mon." I held out my hand. "You were fantastic, Mallory." I couldn't believe the change my friend had gone through.

She hopped down and beamed. "Thanks. Something inside me snapped when Billy told me to leave Zach on the ground."

As the mob dispersed, they stopped to say a word to Mallory or give her a high-five, or slap her on the back. She might be more beat up by her new friends than by Billy.

When everyone else left, Zach faced her. "Uh, thanks. You were awesome." His face turned a dusky red.

Mallory's cheeks flushed and her eyes shone. She stuck out her hand and Zach grabbed it and gave it an awkward shake.

Following the pointing fingers of Andrea's group, Ms. Landau took Zach aside to talk to him.

We walked toward the lunch tables. "What got into you, Mal? I mean, I'm amazed, but it was soooo not you. Do you think your skull had anything to do with it?"

She shrugged. "I don't know. I just couldn't take the bullying any longer. Especially after this morning; I don't want my mom called to school ever again." She glanced over her shoulder as Ms. Landau led Zach into the office. "I hope his ribs aren't broken."

I straddled the bench. "Me, too. I didn't mean for Zach to get caught up in Billy's fall." The words came out of my mouth before I could stop them.

"What are you talking about, Angela?"

She snatched my journal out of the backpack, but I pulled it away.

Mallory crossed her arms and glared at me. "Angela Ashby, what did you write?"

I flipped through the pages and turned the book toward her.

She read my last entry and her face flushed. "You did it again. After I begged you not to?"

"But I wanted to stop Billy. He hit and shoved kids as he passed them."

She pushed the book toward me. "Don't you understand? By tripping Billy, you're no better than he is. You're even more cowardly because you did it from afar."

Whoa. Was she calling me a bully?

"Remember what I said about intention, Angela?" Mallory grabbed her lunch and shoved it in her bag. "When you stop trying to play God with that thing, and understand the consequences, let me know. Until then, I don't want anything to do with you." She stormed off.

"But ... I was only trying to help." The words were said to her back and I doubt she heard me.

A lump formed in the base of my throat and tears pricked my eyes as I watched my best friend in the whole world walk away from me.

Maybe forever.

I hurried out to the athletic field as soon as class finished. I let out a big sigh. Tatiana flittered through the bushes singing while Malachite stalked a bug.

She spied me and flew over. "Hi A, is school over?"

I nodded.

"Where's Mallory?"

"She'll be here in a minute." Whether she'd talk to me remained to be seen.

Mallory sped around the corner and stopped, her face stony.

"M." Tatiana flew a loop the loop and landed on Mallory's head.

"Hey, T. Why don't you get under my hair? We have to run."

Tatiana used Mallory's straight hair like a rope to slide down.

"Mal—"

She put her hand up in front of my face. As soon as Tatiana settled, Mallory turned without saying a word, and walked away.

I saw a flash of glitter in her hair. "Tatiana. Wings."

She pulled her wings in. "Call me T."

Her words floated to me on the breeze. I took a deep breath. I didn't know what I expected. I choked back a sob. I guess it was too much to hope Mallory would forgive me. That wouldn't be happening any time soon.

Malachite rubbed against my ankles so I picked her up and sniffed. "What am I gonna do? My best friend in the whole world won't talk to me ... and all I was trying to do was stop a bully."

Hugging the cat helped calm my emotional storm to where I might make it home before bursting into tears. "I didn't mean for anyone to get hurt." Except for Billy. After one more deep breath and snuggling Malachite tight, I put her down.

Feet scuffing the ground, I shambled homeward. Malachite joined me, but my heavy heart and an empty feeling kept my steps slow and dragging. I'd never walked home from school without Mallory by my side. Well, never when we both went to school and her mom didn't pick her up, anyway.

As I trudged down the street, the happy laughter and conversation of my classmates smacked me from all sides. I swallowed hard. I didn't want to cry where everyone could see me.

Thump.

Billy Shipman jumped over the wall and stood on the sidewalk, blocking my way home.

Normally, I'd be worried about what Billy might do, but not today. Without Mallory by my side, I didn't care if he used me for boxing practice. If I let him beat me up, then maybe Mallory might forgive me. But I couldn't stand in one spot for the rest of the day, so I took a step on to the grass to move around him. He moved with me.

I wasn't in the mood to put up with his games. "What do you want, Billy?"

He took a step forward and put his ugly nose an inch from mine. "You're friends with Mallory, right?"

"Yeah, so?" *Please let us still be friends.*

He braced his arm against the telephone pole behind me, and leaned in closer. "You tell your friend ..."

A puff of his breath went up my nose and my head snapped back. Gross.

"... she needs to watch out. Next time she gets in my way, I'll crush her."

Malachite ran between us and paused long enough to nip at his ankle.

With his attention distracted, I ducked under his outstretched arm and hurried down the grass.

"Hey, Angela."

I turned and put my hands on my hips. "What? You gave me the message." Standing around talking with Billy Shipman of all people was the last thing I wanted to do. I just wanted to go home. "Why did you give it to me? Why not Mallory?"

He hesitated.

"Oh, I get it. You're afraid she'd embarrass you twice in one day. Geez, Billy. Not exactly the way to show you're a tough guy."

I turned my back to him and started homeward again. I half expected to hear his footsteps pounding behind me, but I didn't.

Mallory had called me a bully. After all the times I stood up for her with Cynthia, she knew I hated bullies. It wasn't fair. How could she even think I was the same as Billy and Cynthia?

If Mrs. Clark was allowed to come back to English class, I could use this experience as an example of irony.

Why didn't Mallory understand I only tried to help the kids Billy picked on?

The walk home never seemed so long.

Halfway. I had to stop thinking about Mallory. If I didn't, I wouldn't be able to hold back the tears any longer. But what else could I think about?

Oh, yeah. Dinner with Dad. It didn't exactly bring happy thoughts either. I only agreed to dinner to make Mom happy. I wouldn't be able to get out of it now.

If I pretended to be sick, they'd both know I was faking. And then they'd both stare at me with concern. Parental puppy dog eyes. Enough to give me shudders just thinking about it.

At the edge of the drive, Malachite disappeared into the shrubbery and I stared at the house. With sand colored exterior and hunter green trim, it sat in the middle of a well-kept yard. We used to be happy, all three of us together.

Now? Mom and I were trying to put the pieces back together. Maybe Mallory and I could too.

Chapter Seventeen - Dinner with Dad

"Angela, your dad is here." Mom called up the stairs.

I lay on the bed, my gaze fixed on the ceiling. After today, I wanted the bed to swallow me and take me to a land far away. A land where the rainbows on the comforter were real and you never had to do anything you didn't want to.

No such luck.

Would the journal suspend time? Or maybe I could reverse it? Go back to before Cynthia tripped Mallory and make sure it didn't happen.

"Angela."

If I didn't move, she'd come get me. And neither one of us wanted that. I swung my leaden legs over the side and sat up. I clumped across the room and pulled the door open. Each footstep on the stairs thudded like a bag of wet cement. At least Mom could hear me coming.

When I hit the landing and turned the corner, Dad raised his hand. "Hi, Pumpkin."

I curled my upper lip. "Don't call me Pumpkin. It makes

me sound fat." Did he think I'd forget about him skipping out on me because he called me by a nickname?

Dad exchanged a look with Mom. She shrugged.

"But I've always called you Pumpkin." Hurt filled each word.

I sneered. "I'm not a baby anymore." When he moved out and married Holly-the-homewrecker, he lost the right to use pet names.

Dad stiffened. "You're right, you're not a baby." He cleared his throat. "Where's your jacket? It'll be cold after the sun goes down."

"I'll be right back." I ran up the stairs.

Rushing back down, I heard Mom's voice, but couldn't make out the words.

Exasperation colored Dad's response. "Look, Eva. Don't tell me how to repair the relationship with my own daughter."

I stopped dead. Not even five minutes together and they found something to fight about. It never failed. And that something was usually me. Worse, they'd forget about me while they fought.

I rounded the corner and blew past them to the door. "I'm ready. Let's go."

Anything to stop the fighting. Even going to dinner when all I wanted to do was spend time alone.

I went out the door, down the drive and hopped into the little economy beater Dad drove. Seatbelt on, slumped down, arms crossed, I waited, eyes straight ahead.

Dad opened the door and slid behind the wheel. "Where do you want to go, Pum ... Angela?"

I shrugged.

He turned the key. He cranked it for a moment before the engine caught. "You're going to have to give me more to go on than a shrug."

I braced a foot against the dash. "Wherever. It's your dinner."

The engine idled. "No, it's our dinner. I want to take you someplace you'll enjoy." He put the car in reverse to pull around the car parked in front of us. "Hey, how about the Kid Zone. You used to always love going there."

"Dad, I'm twelve. Not two." Parents could be so exasperating.

He hit a button to open a ceiling-mounted compartment. "Sorry. I can't get used to my little girl growing up." He pulled out his sunglasses and put them on. "Well, because you're so grown up, do you want to try sushi?"

"You want to make things up to me with a special dinner and suggest raw fish? Ew, Dad. That's gross." I barely ate cooked fish, so the thought of raw fish disgusted me.

"I just want to spend time with my best girl." Dad sighed. "They have teriyaki and tempura; you don't have to have sushi. But we can go wherever you want to."

I didn't care where we went. "The fish place is fine."

I turned on the radio and stared out the window as we drove along. Dad had the station set to talk radio. Boring.

When the station went to commercial break, the volume kicked up a notch. "Tired of feeling uncomfortable in a crowd? Struggling to get rid of the itchy, burning sensation and the crusty aftermath it brings? Don't let jock itch ruin—"

Dad lunged for the button to change stations. I kept my head turned toward the window and attempted to suppress my giggles. His face was probably beet red.

He played with the radio stations trying to find something other than the talk show. I didn't know what. After all, it was his car; you'd think he'd have other stations programmed.

Dad finally stopped fiddling with the stations when he landed on KWHZ.

Good grief. He thought he found a station I liked.

I had news for him. No one but young kids and adults trying to act like kids listened to it.

He bopped his head sideways to the beat of the music. "Good beat, huh, Angela?"

Someone please kill me now. I slumped further down in the seat. What if someone from school saw us together? While I sat helpless, a prisoner in his barely functional car, my dad acted like the dork of the century.

"Yeah, it's happenin', Dad." I kept my tone deadpan, hoping he'd pick up the hint.

The restaurant better be close. The shorter the ride, the happier I'd be.

Oh no, he drummed the steering wheel in time with the head bopping. Next he'd start singing along.

My dad. The one-note wonder who couldn't carry a tune in a bucket with both hands. Maybe I'd be spared because he didn't know the words.

Nope. He hummed with the music. Or tried. He sounded like a dying bumblebee in the last throes of an agonizing death. Would he get offended if I plugged my ears?

Too late. He broke out into full voice. With the wrong words.

The sound would worm its way around my fingers anyway. At this rate, it might melt my eardrums. "How far to the restaurant, Dad?" I had to stop the torture.

"What? Oh, we're about five minutes from there."

Great. Now to keep the conversation rolling for five minutes so he didn't break into song again. I reached out and turned the volume knob down. It might help.

"Uh, how'd the Bears do this weekend?"

A light gleamed in his eye. "I'm glad you asked. The Bears trounced the Packers and sent the cheese-heads running back to Wisconsin crying for their mamas."

The words *football fanatic* and Dad went hand in hand. During football season, getting between him and the television when a game was on bordered on dangerous. And the words *it's only a game* were answered with a black look.

"All those clowns who picked the Packers to go to the Super Bowl are looking pret-ty foolish now."

Only desperation could make me ask about football, but between his singing and listening to him ramble about football,

I'd take football every time.

"We went down at the start, and you should have seen the cheese-heads, Ange. They were smug and taunting, wearing their stupid triangle cheese hats."

I stared out the window again. He didn't need anyone to listen to what he said, he just needed to *think* you were listening. But most importantly, he'd rant on about the game for the remainder of the trip to the restaurant, and I'd be safe from hearing him sing again. Until the drive home. But I had time to come up with another ploy between now and then.

We ordered our dinner, and the awkward lull came. That time between giving your order and it arriving at the table. Nothing for you to do, but talk.

And I didn't want to.

I'd already blown my best diversionary tactic on the way. Once the food arrived, I could at least pretend to be engrossed in eating. And it wasn't polite to talk with your mouth full.

Dad unfolded his napkin. "Angela, about this weekend …"

"I get it, Dad. Your new life with Holly is more important. I'm just a reminder of your painful past." I dragged the chopsticks on the table, drawing circles in the cloth.

"Angela, that's not true. You're important to me."

My eyes met his. "Yeah, that's why you've spent sooo much time with me since you moved out." I tried to keep the sneer off my face, but my lip curled. I went back to making designs on the tablecloth with the chopsticks.

"You need to cut me some slack."

My head shot up. "Why should I? You're the one who left. You're the one who hasn't been around, who hasn't made the effort. How else am I supposed to feel about it?"

All the words I'd thought but never said welled up and choked me. "I don't want to talk about this anymore." The gold glint of the restaurant's scattered figurines blurred as tears stung my eyes.

Dad tugged on the end of his mustache.

I'd always been so worried about losing his love, I'd never told him how I felt about his leaving before. But since he didn't care enough to see me when he was supposed to why should I keep silent any longer? I was done trying to make him feel better about leaving.

The server hurried to the table with a pot of hot tea. She turned our cups upright and poured some steaming hot liquid in. "Your gyoza will be right out." She left at a trot.

Ugh. The gyoza could wait. What if I didn't like it? I didn't even know what it was.

I wrapped my hands around the steaming cup. I didn't understand why the cups were so small. Two swallows and it would need to be refilled. But the warmth felt good as it spread through my fingers.

Dad cleared his throat. "So how has school been?"

I raised one shoulder. "Okay."

"Classes going well?"

"Fine."

The server ran up to the table and deposited the gyoza without a word and rushed off.

They looked like dumplings. Maybe they wouldn't be too bad. I contemplated my chopsticks. They were joined at the top.

Dad grabbed his by the bottom and broke them apart. I followed his example. I put a couple dumplings on my plate and poured some soy sauce over them.

Using his chopsticks, Dad plucked up a dumpling and put it in his mouth. He knew how to use chopsticks? I'd never seen him use them before. Maybe he learned from Holly.

I wasn't sure how I'd get the dumpling to my mouth. I took one chopstick and skewered the dumpling. I took a bite.

The savory meat filled my mouth. Delicious. It was still piping hot and I tried to let it cool as I gingerly chewed.

Dad glanced at the remainder of the gyoza on my stick. "Angela, we can get you a set of silverware if you want." He raised his hand in the air. "I'm sorry. I didn't think."

Understatement. I'd never used chopsticks before—at least not successfully—and he should've known. Not thinking seemed to be part of everything he did lately.

Chapter Eighteen - Like Old Times

As I finished chewing the gyoza, the assistant scurried up to the table, plunked a fork next to my plate and rushed away. I put the chopstick down.

Mallory tried to teach me how to use them once, but we laughed at how bad I was more than anything. Maybe I should ask her again.

My throat tightened. Except Mallory wasn't talking to me. At least I had forgotten about our problems for a few minutes. How long would she stay mad?

I cut the dumpling on my plate with the fork. "Dad, why do bullies have to pick on people?" I forked up the gyoza half and plopped it in my mouth.

Dad lowered his chopsticks and rested them on his plate. "That's kind of a hard question to answer. They could be lashing out because they're being picked on. Or they don't like themselves and need to try and make themselves feel better than someone else." He folded his hands and his knuckles turned white. He gave me the parental puppy dog eyes again. "Is someone bullying you, Angela?"

I tucked the meat into the side of my mouth. "No. I don't put up with it."

He relaxed and his fingers and knuckles returned to their normal color.

"But there's a girl at school who picks on Mallory. I've been sticking up for her since the beginning of school. And there's a boy who picks on anyone who's smaller than him." I ate the other dumpling half.

"Do the teachers know about the bullying? They should be doing something about it."

How could the teachers do anything about it when they got in trouble for taking a student to the office? "They try, but it's complicated."

Dad snorted. "It's not complicated, Angela. The teachers are the adults and should be able to deal with a couple teen bullies."

"You don't understand. Things are different than when you were in school." I refilled my small teacup and took a sip.

Dad cocked his eyebrow. "I didn't go to school in the dark ages, despite what you might think. Things can't have changed that drastically."

Our food arrived. A plate of beef teriyaki and tempura sizzled in front of me. Dad's plate had a bunch of different fish things on rice blocks, and a couple round rice things with stuff in the center and a glob of green stuff on the side. No heat rising from his plate at all. And definitely not appetizing to me.

I forked a chunk of hot meat and put it in my mouth. The flavor made my tongue happy. Sweet with a little tang. Yummy.

Dad poured soy sauce into a flat dish and put some green stuff in it and swirled it around with the ends of his chopsticks. He waved his hand over his tray. "Would you like to try?"

I wrinkled my nose. "No, thanks." After crunching a piece of shrimp tempura, I took a deep breath. I needed to talk to someone about what happened today. I couldn't talk about the journal, of course. Dad might think I'd lost my mind if I told him about it. He didn't believe in anything unless he could see and touch it.

"That bully I told you about, tripped Mallory today for no reason, and when a teacher tried to help and told Cynthia she had to go to the office, Cynthia pushed the teacher." The words tumbled out with a will of their own.

"The teacher took her by the arm and escorted her to the office, and now the teacher is in trouble because Cynthia's parents claimed the teacher shouldn't have touched her. It's not fair." Guilt slid into my stomach because I didn't mention the warts I put on Cynthia's nose. But Dad wouldn't understand.

Dad lowered the sushi back to the tray. "The teacher is in trouble for stopping the bully? There has to be more to it than that."

"There isn't. I told you it's complicated." I took another sip of tea. "When Billy Shipman tripped and fell on Zach during lunch, he blamed Zach. Then Billy kicked him and probably cracked his ribs."

Another guilt pang hit me because Billy wouldn't have fallen on Zach if I hadn't made him trip on the planter. But he'd have picked on Zach anyway. "A teacher stood nearby, but she pretended she didn't see what happened because she didn't want to get into trouble like Mrs. Clark did."

Dad took a bite of his sushi and leaned in. "What happened to Zach?"

And then it felt like old times when Dad would come home from work, and we'd chat about our day. I talked to Mom about things, but she never forgot she was a parent and had to point out when things were wrong or right. With Dad it was like talking to a friend. Not quite the same as Mallory, but close. I found myself telling him all the events of the day.

Well, all the events except for Tatiana and the journal. By the time I finished, we were done with our meal and Dad paid the check.

We walked toward the exit and Dad put his arm across my shoulders. "I've missed our talks, Angela. And I'm sorry I don't get to see you as often."

"Whose fault is that?" The words snapped out before I could stop them.

"Honey, don't. We've just had a nice night. Let's not ruin it."

We got in the car and he started it up. "I know you're worried about what happened with Mallory. But you girls have been friends for too long. You'll make up soon."

I danced around why Mallory wasn't speaking to me

because I couldn't mention the journal, but I told him we got in an argument.

I expected Dad to leave once I hopped out of the car. Instead, he turned off the engine and got out. Maybe Mom wanted to talk to him. I didn't stop to ask. Part of me didn't want to know.

I had a big enough mess to straighten out without inviting disaster by getting in the middle of a conversation between them. It never ended well.

Upstairs, I opened my bedroom door only to jump when Malachite mewed at me. My heart raced. How the heck did she get in my bedroom? I scooped her up. I'd better shut the door before Mom knew a stray cat had wandered inside. Although, Malachite didn't strike me as a stray and had never wandered a single moment since I had met her.

Instead of closing it all the way, I left the door a crack open so I'd know when Dad left.

I flopped on the bed and let my legs dangle over the side. Malachite crawled out of my arms and curled up beside me. It irritated Mallory when I used the journal to change things. Maybe I should stop writing in it. From what I could tell, most of the time when I wrote in it, things got all muffed up anyway, so what was the point?

I recalled Madame Vadoma's words to me. *Use it wisely.* Obviously, I hadn't. And if it was supposed to give me great power, it sure didn't feel like it.

I meant to do something good by stopping Billy and

Cynthia from hurting others. So why did it backfire?

Muffled voices drifted up the stairs.

I grabbed my teddy bear, Darlington, and tossed him in the air. He turned cartwheels and dropped back into my hands while Malachite tracked him the whole way.

Maybe if I told Mallory I wouldn't write in the journal anymore, she'd talk to me again. I hated when she was mad at me. But could I give up the journal? I couldn't give it to anyone else. And what a waste to let it just sit on a shelf. Besides, what if Mom read it?

I tossed Darlington up again. Mom didn't snoop intentionally, but if it were here, it could happen. Maybe Mallory would agree to us deciding the journal entries together. Then she couldn't get angry about what I put down, because she agreed to it.

What happened during lunchtime with Billy Shipman wasn't such a bad thing. After all, Mallory faced him down and got half the kids in school to rally around her and chase him off. I think she liked Zach and didn't like him getting picked on. So it was a good thing she stuck up for him. Maybe he'd pay more attention to her now.

The voices below got louder. Mom's broke through and I heard every word.

"I can't believe you didn't tell her."

Fighting again. Over something Dad didn't tell me tonight. He murmured something I couldn't make out.

"She's going to be showing soon. Is that how you want her

to find out?" Disgust colored Mom's words.

Find out what? I sat up.

And what would I be showing? The argument didn't even make sense. Maybe I didn't hear Mom right.

"Nothing is ever good enough for you. You wanted me to make things better with Angela, and I did. Now you're not happy because I didn't break the fragile bridge I built tonight."

When Dad yelled we were about five seconds from the slamming door.

"Greg, you're impossible. You never accept responsibility."

"How long am I going to have to hear it, Eva?"

"Until you grow up."

"Arrgh." *Thud.*

Vibrations tickled my feet. Dad hit the wall? He *never* hit anything, even when they were going through the worst of the divorce.

"Greg, you're bleeding." Mom sounded panicky.

"I'll be fine, Eva." He cleared his throat. "I'll come over Saturday and patch the wall."

"You wouldn't have to if you hadn't decided to put your fist through it."

Slam.

And there it went. End of argument by slamming door. Why couldn't I have parents that got along ... like Mallory's?

I heard the unmistakable sounds of Mom crying, even though she tried to keep it quiet.

When they split, I thought things might get better.

Tonight was worse.

The journal lay on the shelf, tempting me.

I licked my lips as I contemplated it. The urge to write in it became irresistible. I sat up.

One last journal entry and then I'd make things better with Mallory tomorrow.

I flipped through the pages to the first blank one. This was too important to lose on a page with everything else. Malachite leaped from the bed to the desk and sat facing me. She meowed.

Hand trembling, I picked up the pen.

> More than anything in the world, I want my parents to stop fighting and be nice to each other. Why can't they remember all the reasons they fell in love in the first place?

I hesitated. I knew what I wanted to write, but it meant someone would get hurt. Holly. But since she didn't care when she took Dad away, should I care if she got hurt? If this was going to be my last entry, I might as well do it up big.

> I want Dad to sweep Mom off her feet. I want them to get along so well, Dad forgets about Holly. They start dating, get back together, and we

become a family again. And they'll
never fight or break apart ever.

The pen clattered against the desk as it fell from my fingers. Malachite hissed and arched her back. I stared at the entry. What had I just done? A bubble of guilt churned my stomach. But an even bigger bubble of happiness filled me, squashing the guilt.

My parents were going to get back together. We'd be a family again.

Chapter Nineteen - Explosion

I surfaced from my dream heart racing and gasping for air. Perspiration beaded my forehead and pooled at the base of my neck. I sat up and took a few calming breaths. *What a horrid dream.*

It began nicely enough. I had dreamed about my family becoming one again and Mom and Dad being nice to each other and so in love they would never break up again. Malachite had been in the dream too. At first she had been friendly. Mom had agreed I could keep her, so Malachite became a member of the family and we'd go out walking together ... she was my companion everywhere I went.

Then, against a stark white background, I saw Mom and Dad on one side, making lovey dovey eyes at each other, and Holly stood on the other side, alone and crying. Her tears turned into a river with Mom and Dad on one side of it and me on the other. Because they were too busy making eyes at each other, they had forgotten I existed and didn't care I had been trapped on the other side of the river.

At my back stood a deep, dark forest. Malachite grew until she reached the size of a panther. She snarled and growled, baring her teeth which had grown into fangs.

I ran.

Straight into the forest, I ran as fast as I could, hoping the trees would give me enough cover to hide from the monster Malachite had become. Just as she sprang to tackle me, I tripped over a root and fell to the ground.

Then I woke.

Malachite lay at the foot of my bed not moving a muscle. I didn't have nightmares often, but *that* was a doozy.

I glanced at the journal and for a moment the terror I had felt watching Malachite morph into the panther overwhelmed me. Dream Malachite had become a metaphor for my guilt.

I chuckled and a little of the tensions drained away. Mrs. Clark would be proud to hear me use the term metaphor properly.

I had too much guilt weighing down on me. Malachite stirred and looked at me expectantly.

"Let me get dressed and then we'll go to school. I need to talk with Mallory."

Mist hung in the air and dark clouds hovered over the athletic field. The gloom seeped through me as I waited for Mallory. After not sleeping well, I wanted to catch her and make things right. I pulled my jacket closer. The cold oozed into my shoes and slowly turned my toes into miniature blocks of ice. I shivered.

After a few minutes, I stamped my feet to get the blood circulating. My toes felt like they'd break off. How did Malachite stand the cold without turning a hair? My breath made plumes in the air, and I amused myself by trying to make shapes. Mallory should show up any minute to drop Tatiana off before class.

The temperature had dropped thirty degrees from yesterday and it looked like rain. What happened to the warm weather from the weekend?

The bell rang. Where was Mallory? Was she sick? Did something happen to Tatiana? I hurried to my first class; I didn't want to be late.

Yanking open the entry doors, hot air blasted out. My nose defrosted on the way down the hall to class. Good in one way, but now I had a runny nose and I didn't have any tissue and didn't have time to hit the bathroom. Yuck.

By the time I settled in my seat, I'd removed my jacket. Did they need the heater cranked so high? It was cold outside, but the heater spewed hot air into the room at an alarming rate. I glanced around the room. I knew which classmates had been inside the longest by the perspiration sheen on their faces.

By the time roll call finished, sweat beaded my forehead. Was every building this overheated? I'd die before the end of the day. I swiped my arm across my forehead to mop up the sweat with my sleeve. While the weather didn't usually get as cold as today, the school had never tried to roast the students alive.

Mr. Perry wrote on the board and his armpits soaked his shirt and made two huge spots. Disgusting. He stopped mid-sentence and strode to the windows. He threw them open and cold air rushed into the room.

He stood at the window with arms above his head, letting the freezing air dry the sweat on his face. Then he picked up the wall phone and called the office. "It's unbearably hot in here." He listened for a few moments. "When will it be fixed?"

He hung up the phone and wiped his face on his shirt sleeve. Just the few moments away from the window caused the sweat to build again. The bald spot on his head peeked through his carefully combed hair.

When he faced the class, muffled laughter spread. He missed the drop of sweat on the end of his pointed nose.

"Maintenance knows about the problem with the heater and is working on it."

The cold air coming through the window teased me. Puffs of cool mingled with the growing heat, but not enough to help me cool down. I picked up the journal and fanned myself with it.

Anything to get a breeze going. Too bad I couldn't write about the heater and say the problem was fixed and the temperature returned to normal. But I wanted to make up with Mallory and to do that, I had to stop making entries in the journal.

Mr. Perry continued with class, or at least he tried, but then gave up because no one paid attention. Half the class fanned themselves with any object they could find. Those closest to the window concentrated on hogging all the cool air, and the rest of the class slumped in their seats. No one could focus.

My hot face beaded with sweat. Mom used to talk to her friend Hilary about how wonderful it would be to go to a spa and relax in a sauna. If saunas were like this, then the spas could keep them.

Thunk.

Startled, Mr. Perry leaped to his feet and hurried past.

I twisted in my seat. Lindsey Davies, who sat right behind me, lay on the floor with a flushed face. Her eyes rolled up in her head. How freaky. I couldn't look away, but it turned my stomach.

Mr. Perry knelt next to her and spoke softly, trying to rouse her. His head shot up. "Joaquin, go get the nurse."

Joaquin jumped out of his chair and dashed out the door, knocking over the trash can in his wake.

"Desiree, wet some paper towels and bring them here." Mr. Perry rapped the words out.

The beads on Desiree's braids clinked together when her head snapped back. She opened and closed her mouth a few times, but no words came out as she looked at Lindsey's unconscious form. She swallowed hard.

"I need those wet towels."

Desiree stood. "Keep your hair on, Mr. P. I'm gettin' it."

Kids from the outskirts of the room moved in closer. "Is there anything I can get you, Mr. Perry?"

I couldn't see who asked. A pang of guilt hit me. I should have asked how I could help.

"Not right now. Please, just stay back."

Desiree returned and handed a stack of sodden towels to Mr. Perry.

He grabbed them, laid a few across Lindsey's forehead, and draped a couple across her wrists. "Thank you, Desiree."

Lindsey's eyes fluttered. Mr. Perry exhaled and said her name softly.

The room continued to get hotter. If they didn't get the heater fixed soon, we'd all be passed out on the floor. The air burned with each breath.

Banging the door open, Joaquin ushered in the nurse.

"Oh my goodness." She put her hand on her chest. "It's way too hot in here. This room needs to be evacuated." Her head swiveled toward Mr. Perry. "Get the rest of the class outside, and I'll take care of Lindsey."

Mr. Perry struggled to his feet. "Gather your belongings and line up at the door. We'll go out to the lunch tables."

I shoved my things in the backpack, and my chair squealed against the floor as I pushed back. The room, which became quiet when Lindsey hit the floor, filled with rustling, scraping, and murmurs. No one lingered. We all wanted out.

While we made a shambling line at the door, Mr. Perry called the other rooms in the building to tell them to evacuate as well. Then he led us outside.

Walking through the doors to the outside felt like going

from a furnace to a freezer. I couldn't believe I had forgotten how cold it was today.

I plopped my backpack on the lunch table and put on my jacket before sitting. From one extreme to the other. The sweat turned ice-cold as it dried on our skin, making things worse.

Following the evacuation plan, each class had designated tables and we weren't allowed to mingle. Most teachers told their students to be quiet. They almost roast us and we can't talk about it? At least Mr. Perry didn't tell us not to talk. Lindsey passing out must have rattled him.

The nurse escorted Lindsey to the office and the class gave a weak cheer to see her walking.

I glanced around the other tables. Mallory and I weren't in the same class, but we did have classes in the same building for first period. I spotted her head sandwiched between Rob and Justin. I snickered because they were two of the tallest boys in our class and Mallory was one of the shortest girls. The top of her head didn't reach their shoulders. At least she made it to school.

What did she do with Tatiana? Mallory would never be late to class, so she hadn't dropped her off on the athletic field. Then I saw a momentary glint of a wing peeking through her hair before it disappeared again.

Happy to be out of the sweltering heat, the students fidgeted while the teachers discussed their plan of action.

A loud hiss sounded from our left.

Ka-Boom!

Chapter Twenty - Journal Exposed

The ground shook. My classmates' squeals filled the air.

A metal pipe hurtled through the boiler room window. Broken glass tinkled, eclipsed by the clatter of the pipe hitting the ground.

Flames licked the window frame.

Beep—Beep—Beep.

The fire alarm blasted through the campus.

My heart pounded as adrenaline coursed through my system.

Mr. Perry waved his arms over his head to catch our attention. "Line up and follow me."

Once in line, we passed the metal pipe. I eyed it and shuddered. If it had hit someone, they'd have been dead for sure. The pipe pinged as it cooled in the raw morning air.

He led us out to the athletic field, where we were joined by the rest of the school. Each teacher had a clipboard with the roll call on it and again went through the litany of names. Where was Malachite? She had stayed on the athletic field as I had hurried to class, but I didn't see her amber eyes peering out of the bushes.

Black smoke billowed out the broken window and the cloying scent of charred wood grew.

We practiced fire drills every year, but this was the first time I'd done it for a real fire. The drills were almost fun. A chance to interrupt class, get out and walk around. Today the party atmosphere of the drill was absent. Most of my classmates' eyes were wide. No one cat-called or pushed their neighbor.

Sirens sounded in the distance. The wails came closer with each passing moment. The ear-piercing sound cut off mid-shriek. The firefighters had arrived.

Mr. Lassiter led the firefighters to the boiler room.

Jets of water arced through the window. The fire hissed, crackled and popped. The smoke changed from black to gray. The once thick plume thinned until it became a wisp.

The bell to change classes sounded. No one moved.

The urgency in the firefighters died when the water turned off. They reeled back the hose and checked the building for damage.

No longer watching their classes closely, the teachers gathered in a group and chatted. I didn't see Mrs. Clark. My heart sank. Why wasn't she here?

I edged out of line, along with half my classmates, and looked for Mallory in the growing free-for-all.

Waiting for the all clear bell to ring to release us from the athletic field, students formed small groups and chatted in low voices. I maneuvered past several groups before I reached Mallory. She crossed her arms when I approached.

I stopped. "Are you still mad at me?"

She shrugged and made a quarter turn away.

In a word, yes. "I'm sorry. I promise I won't use the journal again." I pulled it out of my bag and held it out. "I'll even give it to you, so you know I'm not writing in it."

She turned to face me, but kept her arms folded.

"Look." I flipped the book open to the last page I wrote on. "I didn't journal anything about the heat in the classroom, even though I wanted to."

"Maybe you should have, Angela." Her tone rivaled the weather.

What? "I'm confused. I thought you didn't want me to write in the journal."

"No." She sighed. "I want you to think about the consequences before you journal."

Her hand jerked out in a tight chopping motion. "When you realized the boiler was out of control, you could have written something to fix the problem. But you didn't."

No fair. "I didn't because I thought you didn't want me to. How am I supposed to keep it straight?"

Angry creases appeared between her brows. "I shouldn't have to tell you."

How maddening. I wanted to make up with Mallory, but she made it difficult. "Okay, Mal. Maybe you shouldn't have to, but I'm confused and I'm trying to get it right. Help me?"

Mallory looked at the sky. "I can't tell you for every situation. You're going to have to figure that out on your own."

That didn't help.

She pinched the bridge of her nose as her eyes watered.

The smell of one of T's farts reached me. The sanitizer must be wearing off.

"But think of it this way ... before you write something ask yourself whether it's going to hurt someone." Her voice sounded nasally with her nose pinched. "It doesn't matter whether you think they deserve it. Simply, will it hurt someone?"

She gazed straight into my eyes. "If it will hurt anyone, then don't do it. If it won't, then go ahead." Mallory pointed at the pipe. "That could have hurt someone and even killed them. You had the *power* to stop it. No one would have been hurt by wishing the boiler wouldn't explode."

Except I didn't know the boiler was going to explode. But I didn't want to argue anymore. "I'm sorry, Mallory. I didn't think of it that way. Thanks for telling me." I inhaled the char-laced-with-fart-scented air. "So can we go back to being friends?"

Mallory finally dropped both arms to her side. "I never stopped being your friend. I was just angry because you weren't thinking." She touched the journal. "This is very powerful. You have to be careful."

Malachite snaked through all the feet of the kids milling around and made straight for Mallory and me.

"Malachite, thank goodness you're okay." I scooped her up

and snuggled her for a moment.

"You named the cat?" Her eyebrows rose. "After my crystal?"

I put Malachite back on the ground so I wouldn't draw attention to her. "She kept showing up and following me, and I couldn't keep calling her cat. She doesn't have a collar or a tag and since she felt like a protector, I named her after your crystal. She likes the name."

Mallory wiggled her fingers at Malachite. "Hello." She glanced at me. "She's a Bombay cat. I looked it up."

Punched in the shoulder from behind, I stumbled and turned to find Cynthia glaring at me.

"Hey, Be-Ash. Gimme that notebook. It's mine." Cynthia reached for the journal.

Malachite jumped between us, hissing and spitting at Cynthia.

I twisted away from her, protecting the journal from her grasp. "Back off. This is mine, not yours."

Cynthia aimed a kick at Malachite who nimbly stayed out of range. "Mangy, flea-bitten cat doesn't belong on school grounds."

"She's not mangy. Her fur is perfect. Unlike your flea-bitten hide." Not my best effort as an insult, but it had the desired result.

Her face flushed and her fingers curled into claws like she wanted to rip my face off. "I'll call animal control to cart that cat off to a kill shelter."

The way Malachite disappeared and reappeared, I wasn't worried about animal control being able to catch her. She could take care of herself. "You're not worried they might mistake you for an ape in a wig and haul you off instead?"

Cynthia lunged for the journal and I skipped to the side.

"That isn't your journal. Just because you've scribbled in it doesn't mean it's yours. Where'd you get it?"

I exchanged a look with Mallory. She faintly shook her head.

"A—It doesn't matter where I got it. B—I could tell you anywhere I liked, and there's no way to prove it. C—I don't have to tell you anyway. It's full of my writing and has my name in the front."

"You stole it from me before I could use it."

Her accusation stung. I'd never stolen anything in my life. Except a pack of gum from the store when I was five. And Mom made me give it back and apologize. My cheeks flushed.

"So hand it over, Be-Ash or I sit on your buddy here and squish her like a bug."

Cynthia's ability to squish Mallory was all too real of a threat, but it's not like I'd stand by and let her. And I couldn't wait for a teacher to overhear her calling me Be-Ash and haul her in to Mr. Lassiter's office for using foul language.

I zoomed away from Mallory and stopped above Cynthia's head. Her little face turned red as she concentrated. I didn't want to call attention to her by staring at her, but I couldn't look away. She drew her knees up then straightened them and flew upward.

Cynthia's nose wrinkled. "Great grief. You two stink. What did you do? Bathe in manure?"

I held back a laugh. T had laid a stink bomb on her.

She held out her hand. "And what have you written in the book that's more interesting than an explosion on campus?"

My jaw dropped. We had been too obvious with the journal. Everyone else was watching the firefighters.

"We're talking about writing up the explosion for the school newspaper." Mallory put her hands on her hips. "And I can confirm the book *is* Angela's because she got it when we were together. So why don't you stop making empty threats leave us alone?"

Mallory? I never thought I'd see the day when Mallory stood up to Cynthia. Billy was different because she had been defending Zach. Watching her, I couldn't regret Billy tripping on the planter. The incident along with her crystal seemed to have given Mallory confidence.

Cynthia's face turned a brighter shade of red and she stepped in and leaned down wart to nose with Mallory. "It's not an empty threat. I'm going to get you when there're not so many people around. Just you wait."

Mallory didn't even flinch. "You don't scare me anymore."

The all clear bell rent the air.

Cynthia took a step back. "I'll be watching."

Tatiana pulled aside the curtain of Mallory's hair and stuck her tongue out at Cynthia's retreating back. "I should have bitten her on the nose." She giggled. "Or her wart, but that would have been gross."

Mallory whispered out one side of her mouth. "T, get back under my hair."

Tatiana slipped back under cover.

I looked around for Malachite, afraid she might be kicked by someone in the crowd, but she had disappeared.

Mallory and I joined the crowd moving toward the classrooms. I wasn't in a rush to get there. My next class was Phys Ed but since most of the period passed while we stood freezing on the athletic field, we wouldn't dress out.

I tapped Mallory's arm. "Quick thinking on the article excuse. Thanks."

Mallory grinned. "That was T. She whispered it in my ear."

"I thought you didn't want to take T into class with you."

"I couldn't leave her outside with it as cold as it is today." Mallory lifted her hand toward the sky. "It might rain, or worse, snow."

I smirked. "It's cold out here, but it's not cold enough to snow."

Mallory scowled. "Well, T is small and she's only wearing a light dress and doesn't have a coat."

"But don't you have some old doll clothes...?"

Phweet. A high pitched whistle interrupted me.

"Will you two stop arguing? I'm nice and toasty where I am, and wouldn't *dream* of wearing someone else's cast off clothing."

Afraid someone heard her, I glanced at the people around us. Fortunately, no one looked in our direction.

"Sorry, T." Mallory patted her on the back with her index finger.

I hitched my backpack higher on my shoulder. "So how did you do in the heat?"

Mallory blew on her hands to warm them. "I became lightheaded, but was more worried about T. I thought she might pass out in the heat and fall off my shoulder."

That would have been hard to explain. And the thought of tiny Tatiana passed out on the floor like Lindsey disturbed me.

We reached the split off point where Mallory would go to her class and I'd go to the gym. "Are we good, Mal?"

Mallory arched her brow. "Are you going to think before you write?"

I practically gave myself whiplash nodding. "Yes. I can't stand for you to be mad at me."

She tilted her head. "Okay. We're good."

Chapter Twenty-One - Evasion

Walking through the door of English, I scanned the room hoping to see Mrs. Clark. My hopes were dashed to find Mr. Farber behind the desk. Why did he have to be here?

I slid into my seat and took out my book. I left my jacket on because the heater was broken. My classmates groaned softly on walking through the door. I don't think anyone was thrilled to see Mr. Farber in front of the class.

It wasn't fair. Why should Mrs. Clark be gone and Cynthia still be in school? She didn't even get suspended a day for tripping Mallory or pushing Mrs. Clark.

Mr. Farber called the class to order and the muttering stopped like someone flipped a switch. He gave us a reading assignment and sat at the desk again. The only sounds in the room were pages rustling, and an occasional creak of the seat as someone shifted their weight. I tried to concentrate on the words, but my mind kept wandering.

Jimmy Simmons drummed his pencil eraser on the desk. The rhythmic sound of the eraser bouncing off the desk surface mesmerized me. Carla sniffed every couple seconds and Xavier kept clearing his throat.

I reread the same paragraph three times, and still didn't absorb the words. I stared out the window. Just a few days ago, a gnome popped out of the bush and waved at me. When I asked for the gnome, I didn't realize how powerful the journal was. And how much responsibility came with it.

If I'd known about the responsibility beforehand, would the journal still be blank?

I thought about what Mallory said. If it was possible to hurt someone by what I wrote, then I shouldn't do it. A drop of guilt slid into my stomach and burned.

My last entry would hurt Dad's new wife, Holly. But she hurt Mom and me first. Didn't that make it okay?

According to Mallory, it didn't. She didn't even like when I gave Cynthia warts for tripping her.

My guilt grew and the snarling panther from my dream filled my head.

But it was already written. I couldn't change what I wrote. And I couldn't undo it. I'd tried with Tatiana, and it didn't work. I curled over my desk and rested my forehead on the edge. What should I do?

"Miss Ashby."

Mr. Farber's voice cut through my thoughts.

"This is not nap time. I suggest you continue your reading."

Snickers rippled through the class, and my cheeks flamed.

I pulled the book closer and started reading again. Before the end of the paragraph, I looked out the window. I couldn't concentrate today. I thought about the gnome again. He didn't stick around, because I didn't have anything for him to do outside of showing up. And he didn't hurt anyone, so nothing went wrong with that experiment.

Same with the unicorn. No one got hurt and nothing bad happened. Things went a little awry with Tatiana, but ultimately Mallory loved having a fairy. Plus she had a living science experiment in her bedroom. And for Mallory, that was close to heaven.

But every time I wrote something that would hurt someone, things went wrong.

Catastrophically wrong.

Mr. Farber leading English class, wrong.

The thoughts chased around in my head, over and over again; my parents getting back together, loving each other and not arguing, Holly getting hurt. Was there a way to fix it so she wouldn't be hurt? Would it help?

Maybe I could have Holly fall in love with someone else so she didn't feel bad when Dad left her for Mom. I reached for the journal. My fingers touched the leather cover then I pulled my hand back.

I'd better think this through to make sure no one else would get hurt before I wrote anything. Maybe I should talk to Mallory about it after school. She seemed to understand how the journal worked better than I did.

A flash of color caught my eye. My head snapped around. I didn't see anything. Everyone else had their head buried in their book. Maybe I should try reading again.

I saw something out of the corner of my eye again. Definitely out the window this time. The branches of the bushes quivered, but there didn't seem to be a breeze. Was a small animal trying to find a warm place to hunker down?

I blinked. Did I just see the tip of the gnome's hat? I rubbed my eyes. Imagination. The gnome left. Didn't he? Plus he wore a flat cap and not the usual pointed hat.

The branches bobbed up and down. Then the gnome's head appeared. He grinned and waved at me. I stared. Why was the gnome back? He had disappeared.

Xavier cleared his throat and I glanced down at my book just in time. Mr. Farber circulated through the room to make sure everyone was reading the right book. He didn't trust us not to sneak another book into the open text book.

He did have a point. Jimmy Simmons sneaked a comic book in once. Mrs. Clark took it all in stride. When she saw the comic book, she asked Jimmy to read aloud. Then she used what Jimmy read to teach us about literary devices.

Thinking about Mrs. Clark, made my guilt over her absence grow. If I hadn't made the journal entry and just let Mrs. Clark take care of Cynthia herself, she'd still be in front of the class, doing what she loved.

What if Mr. Farber came close enough to see the gnome? I turned the page so he thought I was reading the assignment. If he stopped us before the end of class and called on people to answer questions about the reading, I was in trouble. I couldn't remember one word.

Mr. Farber stopped next to my desk and looked over my shoulder at the page number. My fingers tapped on the edge of the book. *The gnome better be hiding in the bushes.*

What if Mr. Farber looked out the window? Would he even recognize a gnome? I bet he'd think it was a little old man wearing a weird hat. But what if Mr. Farber called the police to remove the gnome for trespassing?

I tried not to panic and call attention to the window and turned another page. Mr. Farber moved away to terrorize the next student.

My eyes darted to the window. The gnome's hat bobbed just over the top of the branches.

The bell rang. The tension in my shoulders lifted. I shut my book, shoved it in the backpack and hurried out the door. I needed to talk to Mallory, but first I wanted to discover what the gnome was doing in the bushes.

I waited for the rest of my classmates to head toward the lunch tables while pretending to search for something in my backpack. Once the area cleared, I dashed around the corner of the building then came to a quick halt.

I didn't want to spook the gnome. Since he kept waving and grinning at me, I hoped when I talked to him he wouldn't run away screaming.

As I reached the trees behind the building, I slowed. Maybe

this wasn't the best idea in the world. Maybe I should go get Mallory, in case I annoyed the gnome. I spun on my heels and headed toward the lunch tables.

Mallory would come with me. She hadn't seen the gnome the last time he showed up.

As I looked around the tables trying to spy Mallory, Cynthia glared at me.

Oh, great. Mallory sat one table away from Cynthia. I swore she stalked us. When I stopped next to the table, Mallory scooted to make room for me. I dropped my backpack on the ground and straddled the bench.

Mallory stopped mid chew. "Where's your lunch, Angela?"

I flung my arm toward my backpack but didn't turn my head. "I don't have time to eat." I scanned the tables to make sure no one paid us any attention. Only Cynthia and she looked thoughtful. Everyone else still chattered about the explosion while they ate or pelted food at one another.

I cupped my hands around my mouth and leaned in to whisper in Mallory's ear. Or speak softly. A whisper would never be heard by anyone in this uproar. "The gnome is back and he's behind the English building."

Mallory's head swiveled toward mine and her eyebrows rose. "Really?" She motioned me to bring my head close to hers. "I thought he disappeared the other day."

"He did. I haven't seen him since." My eyes swept the surrounding tables again. "But during reading time I saw him in the bushes."

Mallory arched back, her eyes widening. "Wow."

I leaned closer. "Will you come with me? I want to talk to him and learn why he's here."

I sensed, rather than heard, the flutter of Tatiana's wings. "Angela, quit whispering. You're tickling me."

My head whipped around to see whether anyone heard. I closed my eyes and took a deep breath. Fortunately, her voice didn't carry.

Mallory put her hand on my arm. "Are you sure?"

I nodded. He had to be here for a reason. I wanted to find out.

With scrunched mouth, Mallory packed her lunch.

"Thanks, Mal. You're the best." I stood and slung my backpack over my shoulder.

Cynthia sneered as we walked past her. "So what's the big secret?" She stood and lumbered toward us. "The two of you were whispering nonstop. What gives?"

I matched her sneer. "Like we're gonna tell you."

"I think you're up to something, so I'm gonna follow and find out."

I made a big show of sighing and rolling my eyes. "Geez, Cynthia. I gotta pee. You *really* wanna follow?" I shrugged. "Be my guest." I tugged Mallory's arm and headed toward the bathroom.

Cynthia called after us. "You're so joined at the hip you can't pee alone now?" Her laughter followed us across the quad.

Once inside the bathroom, Tatiana piped up. "M, when

are you going to let me take care of her? She's such a witch." Her squeaky voice bounced off the concrete walls and metal stalls.

I covered my mouth to hold back the laughter. Tatiana and I were on the same wavelength. Someone should do *something* about Cynthia.

"We already talked about this, T. I won't lower myself to her level and I don't want you to either."

Tatiana flew up to the air vent to check whether we could leave without Cynthia following us.

I avoided going in the school bathrooms as much as possible. Hanging out in one made me twitchy.

A cigarette butt floated in one of the toilets and toilet paper wads covered the floor. And the graffiti covering the stalls was nothing like the rainbow-graffiti art I had on my walls at home.

"Okay. Quad is clear." Tatiana zoomed back to Mallory and hid under her hair.

I pushed the door open a crack, poked my head out, and crept out of the bathroom, with Mallory right behind me.

Chapter Twenty-Two - Glimrick

We dashed around the corner of the English building before slowing our pace. I held my arm out to hold Mallory back. "I don't want to scare him."

She nodded.

Moving forward, footsteps slow and quiet, we made our way to the back. At the edge of the building, I stood still.

The bushes rustled and Mallory gasped. I didn't understand why Mallory was so keyed up. For all we knew, it could be Malachite hiding in the bushes getting ready to pounce on us. But at her gasp, the bushes went silent.

Tatiana crawled out from her hiding place and peered into the bushes. She zoomed off.

Mallory reached for her and missed.

At the edge, Tatiana squeaked and flew back to Mallory, wings flashing.

A quivery voice came out of the bushes. "My princess?"

Princess?

Tatiana whispered, a sound barely louder than a leaf hitting the ground. "Don't tell him I'm here."

The tip of a red-pointed hat showed briefly above the bushes then disappeared. Reappearing after a moment, the branches shook and the tip moved toward us. At the edge of the bush, the gnome audibly inhaled and stepped forward.

Malachite came out of another clump of shrubbery and stalked toward the gnome.

"Malachite, no."

She ignored me and continued to move stealthily toward her prey.

The gnome glanced at Malachite. "You'd best keep that beast away from me. Or I won't be held accountable for my actions."

Like I had any control over Malachite.

She stopped about six inches from the gnome and stretched a paw toward him.

He held up his hand and with a crackling noise, a blue light shot straight at Malachite. She hissed and backed up a few paces, then sat and twitched her tail.

Since Malachite didn't appear to be hurt, I couldn't get too mad at him. Besides, shooting blue light from his palms was pretty cool. He faced me again.

His face, wrinkled with age, still had rosy cheeks. His white tufted brows rose in the middle and down at the corners as he shifted his weight from foot to foot. His snowy-white beard covered half his chest, neatly combed and trimmed. What happened to his flat cap?

Oops. I caught myself staring and heard Mom's voice in my head reminding me to be polite. "Hello, little gnome." He came up to my knee, but his hat stretched halfway up my thigh.

"Humph." He frowned and the wrinkles cascaded down his face. "I don't address you as little girl. I do have a name, you know." He crossed his arms.

My cheeks burned. "I'm sorry. My name is Angela and this is my friend Mallory, what's yours?"

"I am Glimrick." His arms dropped to his sides.

A breeze swirled through the leaves. Glimrick lifted his nose in the air. "My princess is near. Where have you hidden her?"

My eyes slanted toward Mallory and she raised her shoulders. She didn't know either.

"Glimrick." Tatiana poked her head next to Mallory's chin. "What are you doing here?" Her tone demanded an answer.

Glimrick bowed so low the tip of his hat touched the ground.

Tatiana, a princess?

"My princess, your mother, the queen, has become concerned with your absence and ordered me to find you." His muffled voice sounded like it had bubbles in it. He straightened.

Tatiana fluttered her wings and paced in midair, arms crossed.

Mallory held up her hand and Tatiana landed, sat cross-legged, and rested her chin on her fist.

He whisked his hat off revealing a small bald patch, and twisted it in his hands. "Might I convince you to return to allow the queen to see you are well?"

Tatiana shook her head. "I can't go back now. Mallory and I are in the middle of an experiment."

Pain crossed Mallory's face. "Um, T? If you have to go, I understand."

"No, M. I'm going to stay with you." She hopped up and faced Mallory. "Remember when you said if I got caught they'd keep me in a jar? Well, that's what my mother wants to do. Keep me in a jar."

Glimrick's hands curled into fists and he stiffened. "Princess Tatiana." His voice shook. "Your mother, the queen, does not want to keep you in a jar."

She looked over her shoulder. "Call me T, Glimrick." Her head spun back. "I should call him G." She giggled and did a flip. "Can I call you G?"

Glimrick ran a hand through his snowy hair. "You may address me as Glimrick, as you have always done. And I shall continue to address you as Princess Tatiana."

She pouted. "Oh come on, G. Lighten up a little."

Before Glimrick could open his mouth, Tatiana snapped her fingers. "I almost forgot. What happened to Nobkin? Why are you here and not him?"

Nobkin? My jaw dropped. This just kept getting more and more interesting.

Glimrick popped his hat back on his head. "Nobkin was

tasked with finding you, but your mother, the queen, felt he didn't exert himself."

He pierced me with his blue-eyed gaze. "You might appear a little less loutish if you'd close your mouth."

My jaw snapped shut and Mallory snickered.

His eyes grew sad. "It didn't help when the sentries found Nobkin sleeping in the toadstool field."

Tatiana's hands flew to her mouth. "Has he been tried yet?"

Glimrick shook his head.

"Good. You go back and tell my mother I ordered Nobkin not to look for me before I left. She cannot fault him for following an express order. And I won't have Nobkin turned to stone and put in someone's garden because he did as I asked." Tatiana muttered and paced back and forth on Mallory's hand.

After a few moments, she stopped pacing. "Glimrick, please return to my mother. Tell her you saw me and I am well, but choose not to come home for now." Her lavender dress swirled in the breeze. "If you need to reach me, you can catch Angela's attention and she will let me know and we will come see you." She waved her hand in the air to indicate the audience was over.

Glimrick raised a bag. "Before I go, I brought you some pennycress to entice you back home."

"You brought me pennycress?" Tatiana zoomed down to him. "It's my favorite."

Glimrick handed her the bag. "You should have something

to remind you of home."

Tatiana threw her arms around him, well as far as she could reach, and kissed his cheek. "You've made me happy, Glimrick." She reached in the sack and pulled out a plant with a white flower just coming into bloom. She took a big bite.

I stepped forward. "Uh, Glimrick? May I ask you a question?"

Glimrick glanced at Tatiana, who waved her hand to give her permission.

He scowled and crossed his arms. "Very well."

"When I saw you before you wore a flat cap, why didn't you wear the red hat then?"

His face brightened. "Ah, perceptive of you. The queen requested that I search for Princess Tatiana in disguise, to eliminate the possibility of capture." He stroked his snowy beard. "I thought about putting together an elaborate costume, but have noticed humans don't pay close attention to what they see. If I wore a simple flat cap instead of a costume, most people would see me as a short, old man, and not the strapping gnome that I am."

I grinned. It was true. The cap made me question what I saw. "It was a good disguise."

He beamed.

Tatiana flew back to Glimrick. "Thank you, Glimrick. This is heaven on a stick. And thank you for your service."

This time Glimrick's shoulders slumped at the dismissal and he turned and walked back in the bushes.

Tatiana landed on Malachite's back and the cat ran around in circles while she stood there like she were riding a circus elephant, all the while chomping her flower.

Mallory stared openmouthed at Tatiana enjoying her flower. Too bad Glimrick wasn't still here to call her a lout.

I nudged her. "Mal. Come on, we should get back to the lunch area before it's over."

I took a step and Mallory grabbed my arm. "Stinkweed."

"What?"

"It all makes perfect sense. I wonder how long the effects take." Her eyes took on the dreamy quality of when she had an idea brewing.

"Earth to Mallory. It may make perfect sense to you, but I'm still in the dark. What are you talking about?"

"I'm talking about Tatiana's fairy farts. I think we've just discovered what makes them smell so bad."

I looked at the bliss on Tatiana's face as she continued to eat the pennycress.

"You're going to break her heart when you tell her."

"I have to confirm, but it makes total sense. Did you know another name for pennycress is stinkweed?"

I shook my head.

"And they've started using it to make biodiesel, too. Being plant based, it makes sense that it gives T gas, and stinkweed is named that way for a reason."

The geeky science girl was in full control of Mallory. Her eyes lit up as she thought through the cause of fairy flatulence.

Tatiana giggled. "Oopsy. Excuse me for farting."

Sure enough the stink bomb reached us moments later. Instead of gagging like she did before, Mallory grabbed her notebook and jotted a few things down.

I grabbed my nose. The stench made my eyes water.

"T, come here for a minute."

Tatiana fluttered back up to Mallory's hand.

"You know the experiments we've been doing with different foods to find what causes you to fart?"

Tatiana nodded.

"I think pennycress is the answer. And that means you won't be able to come to class with me this afternoon. Because you'll stink too much. But it's warmer now, so you can play on the athletic field like before."

Tatiana narrowed her eyes. "You won't forget to come get me, will you?"

"I'm not going to forget. We still have to finish getting your house ready. And we need to find an antidote for the pennycress so you can eat it and not stink."

Tatiana flew next to Mallory's ear as we made our way toward the building with Malachite following behind. When we reached the corner, she hid again to make the trek to the athletic field.

Chapter Twenty-Three - Missing Journal

When I reached the athletic field, Tatiana used the branches of the shrubs like a diving board, bouncing off the end then dashing about. Good thing no one was around.

Malachite tracked her progress and then pounced—missing her. I'd worry about Malachite hurting her, but it was a game for them both.

Moments later, Mallory rushed around the corner. Tatiana waved at Mallory and zoomed off. She became a sparkly glint moving through the sky.

"Hey Mallory, can I ask you something?"

She joined me on the wall. "Sure."

Heat crept up my neck. "Before I understood about not hurting people, I wrote one more journal entry. Now I don't know what to do."

"What did you write?"

I bit my cheek. "That I wanted my folks to get back together so we could be a family again. I didn't think about it hurting Holly." My cheeks turned hot and the memory of the

LIANA GARDNER

panther haunted me because it wasn't exactly true. I didn't care that it would hurt Holly.

Mallory pinched the tip of her chin, which she always did when puzzling something through. "I think it depends on how you wrote the message. What exactly did you say?"

I grabbed my backpack and reached inside for the journal. Huh, it wasn't where I thought. I rummaged a bit more. I didn't see it.

Panicked, I dumped the contents of the bag on the ground. "Angela, what's wrong?"

I spread the books out. "The journal. It's not here."

Opening each book, I shook it to make sure the slim journal wasn't somehow trapped in the middle. "How can it be gone?"

Mallory squatted and helped me look through each book.

"Where did it go, Mallory?" I slumped against the wall, tears ready to fall.

Tatiana returned with an armful of flowers to weave in our hair.

"Not now, T. We have a situation." Mallory handed me the books to put in the pack.

"What's the matter, M?" Tatiana landed on her leg.

"Angela's journal is missing and we're trying to figure out where she lost it."

Tatiana sat in a single fluid motion and laid the flowers on Mallory's leg. "Is that the book the big girl who is always picking on you wanted?"

Mallory and I exchanged a look. Cynthia wanted the book. She thought it was suspicious. What if she took it? But when?

Glasses sliding down her nose, Mallory shook her head. "Forget about that for a minute." She pushed the glasses back in place. "Think about where you've been today and when you last knew for sure you had the journal."

I cast my mind back. Definitely had it through the heat wave and after the boiler blew. I didn't look at it in Fine Arts, so no help there. English class. Seeing Glimrick knocked everything out of my head. But I didn't see him until the end of class time. Did I do anything with the journal before I saw Glimrick?

I rubbed my forehead with my knuckles. *Think.* I closed my eyes and imagined walking through the door. My disappointment with not seeing Mrs. Clark, getting called out by Mr. Farber for putting my head on the desk, and … wait.

I rubbed my thumb against my fingertips, remembering the feel of the leather cover. My eyes flew open. "I had it in English before I saw Glimrick."

Mallory nodded. "Okay, what about after lunch?"

I mentally went through each class and shook my head. "Nope. I never looked for it until just now."

"Was there any place it could have fallen out?"

A tiny bubble of hope sprang up. "Let me think." Tears welled as I mentally went through the afternoon again. "I've got nothin'."

Hanging around the athletic field wasn't going to help us

find the book, so we began the walk home. Tatiana still wanted to adorn Mallory with flowers.

"T, why don't you save those and make a bouquet for your new house?"

"Oooh. I like that idea." She clapped her hands.

On the street in front of the school, a car sped down past and my nose wrinkled in disgust from the exhaust. They must have been doing fifty in a school zone ... someone could get hurt.

"T, take cover." Mallory raised her hand to give Tatiana a landing pad.

The bouquet in T's hands reminded me. "What house?"

She snapped her fingers. "I forgot I didn't tell you. I've taken my old doll house, the one my dad and I built together, and cleared it out. T and I are designing a house for her. It needs a few alterations, but otherwise it's perfect."

"We're even going to put working lights in it." Tatiana ran up to her hiding place.

They had bonded and I felt a twinge of jealousy. Mallory had someone to share things with now, and I didn't. Maybe when my parents got back together they'd give me a sibling. Having a younger brother or sister would be cool. A low growl from Malachite reminded me and guilt churned in my stomach. I had forgotten the hurt to Holly again.

"What am I gonna do, Mallory?"

"I don't know whether there's anything you can do, Angela. If you had the journal, you could try to reverse what you wrote."

"But that hasn't worked before." I couldn't get my mind off the *what am I gonna do* track.

"I know, but you'd have to try. Without the journal, it's impossible. We need to find it."

I was glad of the *we* in her statement. I couldn't do it without her.

After we left the school grounds, Cynthia jumped out from behind a brick wall and stopped us. "Missing something, Be-Ash?"

"Nothing I need from you." I pushed past her.

"Think again." Cynthia hurled the words at my back.

I turned and saw my journal clutched in her dirty paws. "That's mine." The words tore from my throat in a growl.

She smirked. "Possession is nine-tenths of the law."

"Not when you steal it." My arms went rigid.

"Don't worry, once I'm done laughing myself sick over what's inside, I'll black out your name, tear out the pages and burn them."

"Cynthia, please give me the journal."

"Or …?" She arched one eyebrow. "If the pages are funny enough, I'll take pics of them and post them on the internet. Maybe with a few comments thrown in."

I pulled my arm back.

"Go ahead, Angela." She made a come-on motion with her hand. "Hit me so I can pulverize you. I'll be able to say you hit me first, and I won't get in any trouble."

Mallory grabbed my arm. "Just leave it for now."

Cynthia threw her head back and laughed. Then stopped short and narrowed her eyes. "Listen to her Ash-Can and leave it. This book is mine now, and you won't be able to do anything about it."

I buried my face in my hand. Anger burned white-hot inside. How could I walk away knowing Cynthia had the journal?

"Oh, just so you know ... Mrs. Clark is facing the committee tonight, so they can kick her off the staff and take away her teaching credentials."

Cynthia's jeering laugh cut me like knives.

"She'll learn she shouldn't have touched me."

Anger rose from my stomach to my head in a rush. My fingers curled into fists.

A growl rose from the base of my throat.

Mallory dropped my arm and grabbed me around the middle.

I launched myself at Cynthia.

We fell to the ground.

Cynthia's laugh rang out. "You two are pathetic."

I craned my head up, but only saw her legs as she walked away. "Get off me, Mallory."

"Are you going after her?" Her voice muffled against my back.

"No."

Mallory rolled off and sat on the ground.

I pulled myself up. "Why'd you stop me?" Rubbing a hand over my face, I brushed my hair back.

Before answering, Mallory climbed to her feet and held out her hand. I grabbed it and she helped pull me up. We started toward home again.

"I've been thinking a lot about Cynthia lately and why she is so mean. And I think she's lonely."

"Ha. Lonely?" If she was trying to make friends, she needed to get a clue ... badly.

"Think about it, Angela. She never hangs out with anyone else. She always eats lunch alone. The only time she talks to other kids is when she's picking on them."

Mallory was right. She didn't ever hang out with anyone. The only exception was Billy, but even then, she didn't hang out with him. She joined him in picking on kids and when they were done, they went their separate ways.

"But don't you think she'd try to be nice instead of bullying someone into being her friend?" I didn't become friends with Mallory by walking up and slugging her. I asked her if she wanted to be my friend.

She shrugged. "Maybe she doesn't know how."

How hard could it be? Who didn't know how to make a friend? A rock lay on the sidewalk. I kicked it and watched it careen down the street, rolling on to the greenway as it slowed to a stop.

"Well, I don't care. She's mean and I don't like her. I just need to get the journal back."

"But if we know what drives Cynthia, we'll have a better chance of getting it back."

Tatiana poked her head through Mallory's hair. "If you get me close enough to Cynthia, I could put a spell on her and make her give it back."

I forgot that Tatiana could do magic. "That's fantastic, T."

"No magic. We already talked about this."

"But Mallory, we have to get it back. Think about Cynthia reading it. What if she figures out how the journal works?" My arms flailed through the air. "I mean, look at the damage I did with it, and I meant good things ... mostly."

She patted my back. "We'll get it back, Ange. We're not gonna let her win."

Her last words were said with a hostility I never expected, but I still wanted to do something about it now. "Mal, think about how you'd feel if she stole T. Wouldn't you do anything you could to get her back?"

"Of course I'd get her back, but I'd do it the same way."

Although, if I didn't get the journal back right away, my parents would get back together, and I wouldn't have to feel guilty about hurting Holly, because it was out of my hands now.

Malachite nipped at my ankle. Did the cat have the ability to read my mind? I snorted at the thought.

"Angela, I know we don't have time to make friends with her. We have to get the journal back as soon as possible." Mallory stopped and put her hand on my shoulder. "But let's try getting it from her tomorrow by watching her, just the same way she watched us today. Then, if that doesn't work, I'll let T use magic."

"Yippee." Mallory's hair bounced as Tatiana jumped up and down on her shoulder.

My face scrunched up in thought. "Can't I just tell my mom Cynthia stole it and have her get it back?"

"I don't know. It might not be a good idea." Mallory tilted her head to one side. "What if Cynthia denies she took it? You saw her parents. They think she's telling them the truth. And what if Cynthia got spooked and destroyed the journal. Who knows what would happen then? We have to be careful."

She was right. I just wanted to go to Cynthia's house, rip the journal out of her hands, and run.

Why did things have to be so complicated?

We reached Mallory's house and T slipped under her hair. She looked at me with the sun winking off her glasses. "You think of ways to distract Cynthia so we can get the journal back, and I will too. We'll come up with something. Chat tonight?"

I nodded. "See ya."

Even though I still let myself into an empty house, Mom would be home soon. She'd be bubbling over about her new job and I wouldn't be alone for hours at night. Things were feeling more normal at home.

Could Mallory be right about Cynthia? She bullied because she was lonely and didn't know how to make friends? Not that it mattered, because I wasn't going to be the one to teach her how to behave like a human being.

Her parents were odd, too. I tried to image my mom sitting there staring straight ahead and not showing any emotion and utterly failed. Both my parents would want to know what I had done to provoke the teacher. And if they felt I had been wrongly accused, they'd argue with the administration. But no way would my mom say, *'my poor baby'* without reaching out to touch me … or at least look at me.

When I described how Cynthia tripped Mallory, neither one of her parents looked at her. Mine would have given me a glare to end all glares. I'd have wanted to sink through the floor.

Climbing the stairs, I tried to remember what homework I had left. I didn't know how I'd be able to concentrate, but hopefully I'd be able to knock them out before Mom got home.

Unwinding my headphones from my mp3 player, I stuck the buds in my ears and turned it on.

Chapter Twenty-Four - The Big News

With one more math problem to complete, I felt the vibrations from the front door closing. Turning off the music, I yanked the headphones out of my ears.

"I'm home, Angela."

"Okay, Mom. I'll be down in a minute." The last thing I wanted was for her to come upstairs because I brought Malachite in with me. "I'm finishing my homework."

Fortunately, the math problem was easy. Done. I dropped the pencil and skipped downstairs.

Mom smiled at me when I entered the kitchen. "Homework finished?"

"Yep."

"Good job." She pulled a pizza out of the freezer. "Your father will be here in a few moments. He wants to talk with you. Then we're going to the school meeting about the suspended teacher tonight. So you'll be eating solo."

"What meeting?"

"There was an incident where a teacher inappropriately

touched one of your classmates. Tonight's meeting is to discuss the committee's findings and determine what needs to be done."

Panic hit my heart. "Mom, you have to tell them to let Mrs. Clark come back to school."

"We'll have to see what the committee says, Angela." She opened the box and put the pizza on a tray.

Pepperoni. My favorite.

"No, Mom. I was there when it happened. It wasn't Mrs. Clark's fault."

"What happened, sweetie?" She turned the toaster oven on and slipped the tray in.

"Cynthia tripped Mallory, and Mrs. Clark helped her up. Then when she tried to take Cynthia to the office, Cynthia shoved her, so Mrs. Clark took her by the shoulder and escorted her to the office. I swear that's all it was."

"Honey, it has to be more than that. It would be ridiculous to suspend a teacher for escorting a child to the office, especially when the child in question was causing harm to others."

"But it isn't." I wanted to scream. Why wouldn't anyone listen to me?

Mom looked straight into my eyes. "You're sure nothing else happened?"

"Positive. Mallory and I watched them all the way to the door."

She gave me a hug. "Then if Mrs. Clark is not cleared, I'll speak up on her behalf."

I squeezed her back. "Thanks, Mom. I love you."

She laughed. "I love you too, sweetie." She let me go. "It sounds like your dad is here. Why don't you let him in?"

I ran to the door and opened it just as Dad pressed the doorbell. "Surprise."

He reached out and ruffled my hair with the tips of his fingers because the rest of his hand was bandaged.

I looked from the bandage to the hole in the wall and then straight into his blue eyes. "Nice hole, Dad."

The tips of his ears turned red and he cleared his throat. "I'll fix it this weekend." Then raised his hand in greeting to Mom. "You look good tonight, Eva."

Horrified, I watched as Mom blushed.

While I wanted them to get back together, I didn't want to be in the middle of their courtship. Why hadn't I thought about that before I wrote the journal entry?

"Thanks, Greg. I know you want to talk to Angela, so you go on ahead." She motioned with her head toward the couch.

Dad swallowed hard before moving into the family room. He sat on the couch and patted the cushion next to him. "Have a seat, Pumpkin. I mean, Angela." He gave me a sheepish grin. "I'm trying to remember my little girl is growing up. Don't be too hard on me."

I sat next to him and patted his leg. "That's okay, Dad. I know when you get to be an old geezer the memory is the first thing to go."

"Gee, thanks for understanding." He tried and failed to keep his face serious. A smile crept across.

"So what did you need to talk to me about, or have you forgotten already?"

At the reminder, his face grew somber. Uh-oh, this was not going to be a lighthearted discussion.

"I wanted to explain why I wasn't able to pick you up for our usual time together, but you were so upset the other night, I didn't know how to tell you."

"Dad, it's okay. I'm over it." So much had happened, I had almost forgotten about his failure.

"No, you deserve an explanation." He smoothed his mustache. "I had to take Holly to the hospital, and she had to stay overnight. She needed me with her."

Holly was sick? What if she died?

Not that I wanted her to die … but then my parents getting back together wouldn't hurt her. Maybe I was off the hook.

I still needed to get the journal back though. Who knew what Cynthia would do with it.

"What's wrong with her?" My stomach flip-flopped all over the place. I didn't know whether to be upset or happy.

Dad sighed. "That's part of what I need to talk to you about."

Why would Holly's sickness have anything to do with me?

"Holly had to go to the hospital because she was spotting, but it was more than expected."

"Spotting?"

"I'm sorry, she was bleeding. And she needed to get checked out to see what caused the bleeding." Dad took a deep breath. "It was important to find out because Holly is pregnant, and she doesn't want to lose the baby."

Pregnant? "She's going to have a baby?"

"Yes. You have a little brother on the way."

Whoa. "I'm going to be a big sister?" My mind didn't want to take it in. "How did that happen?" I blushed. "I don't mean how specifically."

I leaned back on the couch. "I don't know what to say." My mind froze. More than not knowing what to say, I didn't know what to do. What about my journal entry to get my parents back together? I didn't know about a baby then. I still wanted my parents back together. But what about the baby?

He patted my leg. "You don't have to say anything. But I wanted to let you know the *only* reason I missed my time with you was for something important."

"I'm going to have a baby brother." I said the words to try them out. They felt strange on my tongue. "Does Mom know?"

Dad laughed. "Yes, your mother knows. And I want you to know, that our having a baby doesn't replace my love for you. He's going to look up to his big sister and think you're fantastic."

I didn't feel fantastic. In fact, I felt pretty lousy.

He could count on my having his back if anyone tried to pick on him. I knew how to handle bullies pretty well. I got too much practice with them. And I could help him with his homework when he started school. And how not to throw a ball like a girl. My mind raced with all the other things I could share with my brother.

Then a thought hit me. "But he'll live with you and Holly and I live with Mom. He won't know me."

He draped his arm across my shoulders. "Honey, I promise you, he will grow up knowing you. We'll make sure the two of you are involved in each other's lives."

I gazed into his eyes and the trust I thought I'd lost in him came flooding back. "Do you know his name?"

"We have a few names picked out, but haven't decided, yet. I'll let you know as soon as we do." He glanced toward the kitchen. "Maybe this weekend, you and Holly can go over the names."

"Really?" Not that I would have the final say, but it'd still be cool to be part of picking out my brother's name.

My brother. It sounded strange. After twelve years of being an only child, having another sibling would take a little getting used to.

Mom carried the steaming pizza out of the kitchen and set it on the table. "Angela, I have your dinner ready." She grabbed her purse from where it hung on the corner of the chair. "Greg, we need to get going now."

After Mom and Dad left, I had my dinner, grabbed the remote, flopped on the couch, and turned on the TV. I flipped through channels, not finding anything I wanted to watch. My brain still felt frozen. I was forgetting something.

Oh. I needed to figure out some way to get the journal back. The you're-going-to-have-a-baby-brother thing blew it out of my mind. And now it was more important to get it back than ever. Asking Cynthia would be pointless. But she'd bring it to school if for no other reason than to taunt me. Or lording it over me about how she had read what I wrote. Maybe even make fun of me for the gnome and unicorn.

But how would we get it back? Mallory was right. We needed something to distract Cynthia while one of us stole it. We'd need to follow her to see where she stashed it. And then we'd need a way to get her attention on something else.

A diversion. But what?

A fire always got people's attention, but I didn't think Mallory would let me start a fire. Part of the school might burn down. And we didn't want firefighters to come out to our school two days in a row. Too bad the boiler already blew. That would have been a perfect diversion.

Throwing Zach in the path of Billy Shipman would create a diversion too. But Mallory liked Zach, as much as she might deny, and it wouldn't be fair for Zach to be picked on again this week by Billy. And I didn't know whether Billy would pick on him after the way Mallory faced him down in public.

So far I had no useful ideas. Maybe thinking about something else would let the ideas start flooding in.

A brother. I was going to have a baby brother. The idea astounded me. And I'd have to make sure I was part of his life. Despite Dad's assurances, maybe Holly wouldn't want me to be around him. Would Dad be able to stand up against her?

Then it hit me. If I didn't get the journal back, and Mom

and Dad got back together, Holly might move away with my brother, and I'd never see him. He wouldn't know who his big sister was.

At least he wouldn't know it was his big sister who ruined his life.

But I couldn't let that happen.

The hurt I felt when I learned Mom and Dad were getting a divorce ripped my heart in two. It was the most awful moment of my life. But I had almost twelve years with two parents. I hated not having a dad full time, so how could I take my brother's dad away before he even arrived?

But I missed my dad and I wanted us to be a family again, and I wanted Mom and Dad to get along.

How could I want two things that were so different? If I did nothing, my parents would get back together, and I'd be in a happy, loving family again. Something I wanted more than anything.

Until now.

If I learned how to reverse the spell and Dad didn't leave Holly, my baby brother got the life I wanted; a family with both parents living in the same house. But I'd have to get the journal back first.

I needed to talk with Mallory to see what she thought. I slapped my forehead. I forgot we said we'd chat tonight.

I ran up the stairs to my room. Malachite meowed as soon as I opened the door. *Oops.* I had forgotten she was in my room.

I flipped on my computer and while I waited for it to boot

up, I ran downstairs and grabbed a can of tuna and a little bowl with milk. I made it back up before the machine had fully booted. Why did it have to take so long? Even after the desktop appeared, I still had to wait for all the processes to start. If I tried to click something too soon, it slowed everything down.

Calling would be faster. But Mallory's parents might listen in, and *no one* could know about the journal. Especially adults.

The network connected. Finally. I brought up a chat window.

Hey RU there? Can U chat?

I stared at the blinking cursor and waited for a response.

After a few moments, the status changed to typing. I exhaled and waited.

Mallory usually responded quickly. She must be writing a book.

Finally, the screen flashed.

hi. it's t. i'm typing. wheeeee.

My life reached epic crisis mode and Mallory was teaching Tatiana to type? I wanted to pull my hair out.

Fingers trembling, I typed my response.

That's great, T. But I need to talk to
Mallory.

I hit send.

The cursor blinked twice before the status changed to typing.

What's up?

Relieved, I grabbed the keyboard.

We have to get the journal back
tomorrow.
We'll get it back. Don't worry.
You don't understand. It has to be as
soon as possible. Things got worse.
Holly is going to have a baby. I'll
have a little brother.

The cursor blinked on the screen while Mallory thought through the implications.

Um ... wow. Complicates things a
bit.

I gave a short laugh. I had to choose between ruining my life, or that of my unborn baby brother, and oh, by the way, don't hurt anyone in the process and Mallory thought things were a *bit* complicated.

My screen flashed again.

The plan remains the same. Get the
journal back first, which means
distract Cynthia long enough to
grab it.

But how did we do that?
Thinking.

Mallory waited a few moments then her words flashed.

Any ideas yet?
I thought about fire for a diversion,
but ruled it out. Too risky.
Be serious. We need something
simple but effective.

But what?

Keep thinking. G-T-G.

Mallory's status flashed to offline. Her mom must have come in.

I flopped on my bed and stared at the ceiling. Simple but effective. Easy to say, but hard to think of. Malachite hopped on the bed and meowed tuna breath in my face.

I gathered her into my arms. "What am I going to do?"

Every idea that popped into my head had to be discarded for one reason or another. I couldn't plan anything to hurt anyone or get someone in trouble. In fact, the only thing that might remotely work was for me to pick an argument with Cynthia during lunch and hope Mallory could steal the journal while we verbally duked it out.

She might not suspect us of trying to get the journal back, because as Mallory pointed out, I liked to bait Cynthia. I'd done it often enough before.

But those times it happened naturally. What if she didn't do anything for me to attack? What would I say? Would I have to start the fight? Usually Cynthia started and I finished it.

The sound of a car pulling into the driveway roused me. I glanced at the clock. Wow, Mom and Dad had been gone longer than I expected.

Chapter Twenty-Five - Battle Plan

I crept out my door and halfway down the stairs and sat listening. The front door opened.

"Thanks for driving, and thank you for dinner."

I heard the rumble of Dad's voice, but couldn't make out the words.

Mom laughed. "Yes, it *was* nice to spend time together without arguing. We'll have to do it more often."

Was that the sound of a kiss? Hopefully just a peck on the cheek. Anything more would be disgusting. I forgot the physical part of Mom and Dad getting back together. How embarrassing.

"Goodnight, Greg. And thanks again." The front door closed and I heard the bolt snap into place.

I ran down the stairs.

"Hi, honey. I'm going to make some coffee. Would you like some cocoa?"

I followed her into the kitchen. She must be in a good mood to offer cocoa again. This was becoming a habit. "Sure."

I waited while she prepped the coffee and put the kettle on.

"How did the meeting go?"

"Give me just a minute."

The hot water hit the coffee grounds, and the aroma permeated the air. Coffee smelled so good, but I didn't like the taste. Too bitter.

The only time I liked coffee was as a little girl with my Grandpa. He made it for me in a demitasse cup. He'd put a little bit of coffee, fill the rest with milk and stir in a spoonful of sugar or two. The spoon barely fit in the cup.

When I visited him, I'd wake up early and sit at the kitchen table on top of the white stool with a green vinyl seat, my head barely over the tabletop. He'd make the coffee, whistling and jingling his keys. I felt so grown up drinking coffee with him. It was our secret while everyone else was still in bed asleep. I missed him.

Mom carried two steaming cups to the table and set them down.

I took a sip and enjoyed the smooth, velvety texture of the cocoa on my tongue. It had the right amount of sweet, and warmth spread through me when I swallowed.

Mom arched her brows. "Well, are you ready to hear about the meeting?"

"More than ready." And a bit nervous, to tell the truth.

"The committee explained the process they have to go through each time there is a complaint." She smiled. "And just when everyone in the audience started getting antsy and moving around in their seats, they said in the opinion of the committee

Mrs. Clark did no wrong and would return to teaching tomorrow."

"Yes." I did a fist pump in the air.

Her smile lingered. "That's when things got a bit interesting. The Benson's were there and they objected to the committee decision. The committee had to listen to their complaint and they twisted the occurrence, so several people muttered about sending a teacher who hurt children back to school."

I stirred my cocoa. This didn't sound good.

"I waited until the Benson's ran out of things to say then jumped up to address the committee. Actually, I talked more to the audience than to the committee."

Mom tucked a lock of hair behind her ear.

"I told them what you told me then asked the committee why a teacher had been removed from school for attempting to protect a student from harm, while the student in question, who from all accounts tripped a classmate and pushed the teacher, was allowed to remain."

Yes! "You rock, Mom."

She grinned. "Next Mrs. Chan sprang to her feet and said she wanted to know the same thing. That her child was the one tripped and her version of what happened tallied with what I said."

I wished I could have been there to see it all in person.

Mom's spoon clinked against the cup. "And she wanted to know exactly what the committee and the school were going to do about the obvious problem with bullying on campus."

I took another sip of cocoa and grinned until my cheeks hurt.

"By this time, the Benson's were looking for the nearest exit, and the crowd furor changed from being with them to against them."

They were probably afraid a lynch mob would form.

"And the committee advised they would review the case to determine the appropriate disciplinary action for bullying. My guess is your classmate Cynthia is about to be suspended."

My smile vanished and my eyes widened. "When do you think they'll suspend her?"

Mom shrugged. "Probably tomorrow."

Holy mackinole. I couldn't afford for her to be gone from school for a week. Or even more because she had pushed Mrs. Clark.

It'd make it harder to get my book back. Even if I told Mom about Cynthia stealing the book, because she made the Benson's look so bad at the meeting, they wouldn't even talk to her now and would probably gloat that their daughter had stolen something from me. What if they made the decision tonight and Cynthia didn't even come to school tomorrow.

A horrible thought hit me. What if she were expelled? Or what if her parents decided to pull her out of school? What if I never saw her again?

A sick feeling washed over me. On any other day, I'd have been happy to never lay eyes on Cynthia Benson again ... but today? The thought of never seeing her again made me want to hurl.

"Is something wrong, sweetie?" Mom's concerned eyes didn't leave my face.

How much should I tell her? "Um, not really. Cynthia has something of mine, and I wanted to get it back from her tomorrow. If she's not at school, I won't be able to."

Mom tilted her head. "I'm surprised you let her borrow anything of yours. Or did she borrow it before she tripped Mallory?"

I focused on stirring my cocoa. "Not exactly." I couldn't lie to Mom.

"Not exactly?"

When I didn't answer, Mom didn't push, she patted the back of my hand instead. "I doubt anything will happen before school starts. So find her first thing and if she doesn't return what's yours then we'll go to the Benson's tomorrow night and get it."

"Okay." I'd have to hope not only that Cynthia was at school tomorrow, but that she'd be there long enough for me to get the journal back.

Mom took a sip of coffee, then drummed her fingers against the cup. "I want you to know your father and I had a nice time, too. After the meeting, he took me to dinner, and we chatted like old times." She smiled. "It was nice to spend time with him where we weren't arguing about something."

"That's good, Mom. I'm glad you had a good time." Well,

sort of.

I didn't know what I wanted anymore.

Mom set her coffee cup down. "I think we could talk without arguing because he finally told you about the baby being on the way. How do you feel about it?"

I picked at my cuticles. "I dunno. Happy, excited, confused." The last word slipped out. I didn't mean it to, but I had too many emotions for one person to make sense of. About the baby? Happy and scared. Having a brother would be a dream come true. But I might not be able to undo what I had written in the journal, so I was afraid I had ruined everything.

Use it wisely. Ha! I had been selfish, and worse, I had deliberately written something to intentionally hurt. So add shame to the list of emotions coursing through me.

"We're all going to work together to make sure you have a good relationship with your brother."

But what about her? Would she feel left out? "Aren't you hurt by Dad having a baby with someone else?" The words tumbled out before I could stop them. I couldn't look her in the eye.

Mom stirred her coffee while she thought out a response then laid the spoon down on her napkin. "I was hurt when your father left me. I'm not going to lie to you, but we weren't happy together, and hadn't been for quite a while. He's happy with Holly, and they're making their life together."

She folded her hands and steepled her thumbs. "And, believe it or not, I want him to be happy. He gave me the most precious thing in my life. You."

Her eyes filled with tears. "And whatever the reasons we didn't work out, I want you to have a good relationship with him. He's your father, and that won't ever change."

She looked at the clock and dashed the moisture from her eyes. "You'd better finish your cocoa now, and get to bed." She reached out and brushed the bangs out of my eyes. "And Angela, anytime you need to talk, I want you to talk to me. It doesn't matter what it's about. I've missed our conversations."

Guilt raged like a beast inside me. I finally had my mom back and I had missed our chats so much. But what would she think of me if she knew what I had done? Would she hate me?

The sun shone through the curtains, waking me. At least the day wouldn't be as gloomy as yesterday. Unable to fall into a deep sleep, I had tossed and turned through the night. My mind refused to quiet down.

It would be so nice just to stay in bed today, so I lay there for a few moments. But I needed to face the day. The goal? Get the journal back. Nothing else mattered.

Once I had it back, I'd have to figure my way out of the mess I'd created. But I couldn't do anything without it. Game plan ... get it back before school. If not, then during lunch. Those were my two best opportunities.

I felt sick to my stomach and didn't want to eat breakfast.

Mom watched me carefully. I tried to act as if nothing was wrong.

"Angela, are you feeling all right?"

And failed miserably. "I didn't sleep well. That's all."

"Do you need to stay home from school today?"

"No, I'm fine."

She eyed me suspiciously. "If you say so."

I finished breakfast as fast as possible so I could get dressed and away from her watchful eye.

Mom dropped me off at school before the other kids. I sat on the planter and waited for Mallory to arrive. I hoped she'd come up with an idea, because baiting Cynthia was the best I had.

I no sooner thought of her and the devil appeared. Cynthia approached the school entrance. Would I be able to distract her and steal the journal at the same time? My stomach knotted in about sixteen places

More kids arrived, and teachers made their way to their classroom.

When Cynthia saw me on the planter, her eyes lit up and her mouth curved in an evil grin. She moved in a straight line toward me, glanced up, and stopped. The smile vanished from her face, replaced by a frown.

I peeked over my shoulder and saw Mrs. Clark giving Cynthia a steely-eyed stare, one I was glad wasn't directed at me. A few of my knots unwound. Mrs. Clark wouldn't leave until the threat was gone.

Mallory came up the steps behind Cynthia and gave her a wide berth. She joined me on the planter.

Cynthia glared at us, her face flushed, and she stormed off.

There went the first opportunity, but I couldn't bait her in front of Mrs. Clark anyway.

Mallory waited until Cynthia was out of earshot. "Did you think of anything?"

"Not really. Did you?"

She shook her head.

"We'll have to try the only thing I came up with, which is during lunch I'll purposely pick a fight with her, and you can steal the journal."

Mallory frowned. "I don't know whether that will work. She'll be watching me. Maybe we can get someone else to steal it while she focuses on us. The two of us can distract her better than one."

I thought for a moment. "That just might work. Who can we trust?"

A blush colored Mallory's cheeks. "We could ask Zach. He's been extra nice to me since the Billy Shipman thing."

The urge to tease her about Zach swelled, but I bit my tongue. If I teased her, she might get funny about asking him to help. And I needed all the help I could get.

"Sounds like a great idea, Mal. You ask him and we'll plan it for lunchtime. I'll try to figure out something to pick a fight with her on. Other than the journal."

"The good thing is she does have the journal with her. Her

backpack wasn't zipped all the way, and I saw the corner of it."

Relief flooded through me. My knees even felt weak. Good thing I wasn't standing. Talk about being uptight. Though I still felt sick, a glimmer of hope appeared. I might be able to fix the mess I had made.

The first period bell rang and we parted ways.

When the bell rang for lunch, I couldn't wait to get out of the classroom. As happy as I was to walk into English and see Mrs. Clark back where she belonged, until I got the journal back, I couldn't concentrate on anything else.

My heart beat rapidly and my breaths were short and fast. I needed to calm down or I'd hyperventilate. Although, if I passed out in front of Cynthia, it might create the distraction we needed to get the journal back.

I met Zach and Mallory at the lunch tables.

"I told Zach what the journal looks like so he knows what to grab." Mallory leaned over and whispered in my ear. "And T is on the athletic field so she won't get in the way."

Zach pulled his lunch out and put it on the table. Bologna and cheese with chips and an apple on the side. "Do you have a plan B if I can't get the journal out of her bag?"

Plan B? We barely had plan A. "Um, you're it."

Zach grabbed his chin and closed his eyes. A moment later, he opened them. "Got it. If I can't nab the journal out of her pack, then I help Mallory up on the lunch table and she rallies everyone like she did with Billy Shipman and we get the whole school telling Cynthia to give it back."

Mallory's complexion paled. "I'm not sure I can do it again, Zach. I wouldn't know what to say."

Zach waved his hand through the air. "You were fantastic. The words will come to you."

Mallory's eyes widened. "Let's hope we don't have to."

Chapter Twenty-Six - Rescuing The Journal

The lunch tables filled with our classmates, and still no Cynthia. What if they'd already suspended her and sent her home?

Someone clopped the back of my head. I fell forward and squished the sandwich I hadn't been able to eat as I caught myself before I dove off the bench.

Cynthia's laugh rang out. "Not so tough when no teacher is watching, are you?"

I took a deep breath and prepared to battle. At least she hadn't been sent home yet. Maybe we could help her on her way.

"Sneaking up from behind?" I let a burst of air escape between my teeth. "Coward."

Her laughter changed to a snarl. "What did you call me?"

I stood and faced her across the lunch table. "I called you a coward."

Out of the corner of my eye, I saw Zach move away from us.

"It's what you call someone who picks on people smaller than they are."

Cynthia's fists curled.

"I looked it up in the dictionary and they had your picture there."

Cynthia swung her fist. I danced out of the way. Hindered by the table, her punch fell short. She moved around the table.

The kids around us whispered to one another.

Cynthia came closer. I tried to stay out of arm's reach, but moving backward through the lunch area was like dancing through a minefield. I didn't know when I'd trip over a table or someone's bag on the ground, but I couldn't stop to look.

Cynthia cocked her fist back and lashed out at my head. I ducked and ran behind her.

"Fight!"

I didn't see who yelled, but it was a couple tables from where we were.

More kids took up the cry of *fight*.

Cynthia turned to chase me and her eyes got wide. She lunged, but not at me.

I spun around. Zach. At least he had the journal in his hands.

The crowd chanted. *Fight—fight—fight.*

Zach edged around a table, trying to put obstacles between them.

I pushed through the crowd. If I took the journal from him, she'd focus on me. I didn't want to be responsible for Zach getting hurt again. I had learned my lesson. I didn't want anyone to get hurt because of me.

Mallory got there first. She grabbed the journal and instead of running away, jumped on top of the table.

Where were the teachers? Shouldn't someone have noticed the commotion by now? We'd have to handle this ourselves.

I sprinted and reached the table before Cynthia could and stood between her and Mallory. She'd have to go through me before I'd let her hurt my friend.

Mallory held the journal over her head with both hands. "Quiet!"

I'd never heard Mallory yell so loud before. Shushing replaced the chanting.

Plan B coming up.

"This notebook was stolen from my friend, and Cynthia refused to give it back. Are we going to let her get away with it?"

A universal cry of *No* rang out.

Finally, I saw adult movement on the fringes of the crowd. Again, Mrs. Clark waded in, but this time she had back up. Mr. Perry followed her.

Kids moved to the side to allow them to come through.

Mrs. Clark arched an eyebrow. "Miss Chan, please have one of your friends help you down. I don't want anyone to get hurt."

Zach reached up and offered Mallory a hand. She grabbed it and stepped down to the bench, and hopped to the ground. She handed me the journal.

I felt ridiculously relieved to have it in my hands again. I couldn't open it to see what Cynthia had done to the inside. Like cut out pages, or mark things with black ink. At least not until there were fewer eyes watching.

Mrs. Clark folded her arms. "Thank you. Now Miss Chan, please explain what you were doing on the table."

By the glint in her eye, she knew exactly what she was doing. She wanted someone to tattle on Cynthia, but she didn't want them to be shunned for doing it. Mallory didn't have a choice.

Mallory took a deep breath. "Cynthia stole Angela's notebook and wouldn't give it back. Then she hit Angela and tried to pick a fight with her."

Mrs. Clark scanned the crowd. Several students nodded. She turned to Mr. Perry. "Well, it seems Miss Benson has earned herself another trip to the office." She held her arm out. "This way Miss Benson. And let's not have a repeat of last time."

Cynthia's face scrunched up like she was trying to hold back tears when the crowd cheered.

It was almost enough to make me feel sorry for her.

Almost.

I clutched the notebook to my chest. I couldn't believe I had it back again. I looked from Zach to Mallory. "Thanks so much. You don't know what this means to me." Well, Mallory knew, but I doubt even she realized how important it was to me to get things fixed as soon as possible. I hadn't had a chance to tell her how well my parents were getting along.

Zach eyed the journal. "It must be important for you to go to the lengths you did to get it back."

I couldn't tell him why it was so important, but I felt I owed him some sort of explanation. He put himself in harm's way to help me out. "It is important, to me. It's my journal where I write my private thoughts. Just think of what Cynthia would do with those."

Zach nodded. "I totally understand."

"Thanks again for getting it back for me. I couldn't have done it without you."

I hugged Mallory. "And you are the best friend. *Ever!*"

When I released her, Zach jabbed her lightly on the shoulder. "Mallory is the best."

Her grin was so wide, her eyes narrowed into slits.

Mallory and I met on the athletic field after school let out. She needed to collect Tatiana for the walk home and I wanted to look at the journal with no one else around.

Expecting the worst, I opened the cover. No black marks. Even the name wasn't inked out. I thought for sure she'd black out my name and write hers in, so when I accused her of stealing it she could say her name was in the front.

I flipped through the pages.

"Well? Did she do anything to it?"

"No. It's weird. I thought she'd put something in the

journal. Or tease me about what's inside. Something."

Mallory looked at the sky. "I have an idea. Hand it to me."

I gave her the journal. Malachite snuck out of the bushes and joined us.

Mallory opened it, flipped through the pages and smiled. "I don't see anything."

"What do you mean? I have pages filled with writing."

Her grin widened. "I know, but the only thing I can see is your name in the front."

"But you saw the writing in there before. How come you can't see it now?"

"I think there's a charm on it. I saw the writing because you held the journal. The writing is revealed to the owner of the book." She tapped her index finger against her lips. "I have another idea, hand me a pen."

Bewildered, I grabbed a pen and gave it to her. She scribbled on the page, then flipped to the back and scribbled some more.

"Here." She handed the journal back to me. "It wouldn't let me write anything either."

I opened it. My familiar scrawl greeted me. I flipped through the pages. No scribbles, nothing but my own writing.

Mallory peeked over my shoulder. "I can see the writing now."

Understanding dawned. "Cynthia never saw a single word of what I wrote, so she doesn't know the journal is magic." My lips puffed out from the force of my breath. "What a relief. Even though she's in trouble, I was afraid she'd start making noises about what she read."

Mallory giggled. "Just think of her confusion when she opened it and saw nothing there and couldn't write in it. She saw us talking about stuff on the page."

I stared at my last entry in the journal. My heart sank. "Mal, what if I can't undo this?"

She patted me on the back. "I think you can, Angela. I've been thinking about how it works and all the things you've done with it."

I lowered my voice so Tatiana wouldn't hear me. "But when I tried to make you-know-who go away, I couldn't."

"You didn't want her to go away, though. You were laughing too hard. Think about it, what about your mom's job?"

I thought for a moment. "I made her lose her job."

"Yeah, but when you wanted her to get another one, a better one, she did."

Oh yeah.

"So I think it works based on how much you want something. The only question is do you want your parents to get back together more than you want your baby brother to have a two-parent family?"

I sat stunned. It wasn't enough for me to write it. I had to mean it.

She put her hand on my shoulder. "It's up to you."

I grabbed a pen. My hand hovered over the page. I wanted Mom and Dad back together, but I didn't want my brother to grow up without a father. I closed my eyes and hoped my heart would give me the right words to put down. I took a slow breath in and exhaled.

And then I knew.

Journal, I don't know if you can ignore what I wrote before, but I'd like for you to forget putting my parents back together. I didn't know some things at the time I wrote it which change how I feel. So if you can erase the bit about my parents getting back together. I know what I really want.

I want my parents to get along. I don't want them to fight anymore. I want us to be able to have family get-togethers without tension. I want my dad to stay with Holly and be there for my baby brother. I want to be close to my brother. I want to be a good example for him and someone he can be proud of. And if it means it will help make things better for Dad and my brother, I want to get along better with Holly. Help us to be an extended, but happy family.

I put the pen down and stared at the entry. "What do you think, Malachite?"

She put her nose next to the page, almost as if she were reading it, and purred.

I moved the book over so Mallory could read it.

She grabbed my arm.

I stared.

The entry about my parents getting back together faded and disappeared.

A smile spread across my face. "It's time to get T and go home."

I opened the door of the empty house. Funny how much a few days can change things. I used to dread coming home to an empty house, but now it was for a couple hours and Mom would be home. Things were finally settling into a routine, and one I could live with.

After I wrote the journal entry, my heart lightened. Things were going to be better. Mom and Dad would be nicer to each other, I'd get along with Holly, and I'd have a wonderful baby brother who would look up to his big sister.

The phone rang. "Hello?"

"Hi, Angela. It's Holly."

Why would Holly call me?

"I'm glad you're home from school. I want to go shopping for some baby things and wanted to know whether you'd like to go with me. I've already cleared it with your mom."

Holly wanted me to go shopping with her?

"That'd be cool."

"Fantastic. I'll be there in about ten minutes to pick you up."

I hung up the phone and ran upstairs with Malachite at my heels.

Pulling the journal out of my backpack, I carefully placed it on the bookshelf. I didn't want anything to happen to it ever again. I still had no idea why Madame Vadoma gave it to me. And there was no question it was meant for me because my name was inside. Why was I destined to have great power?

I glanced at Malachite. She stared directly into my eyes.

"All in due time ..."

My mouth popped open. I could have sworn I heard Malachite speak to me.

She blinked, and I heard words again.

"All in due time ..."

A Note From the Author

Dear Reader,

When I was twelve, I remember having plans and dreams … things I didn't want to share with anyone for fear someone would try to talk me out of it or worse, tell me it was a stupid idea. I have always loved making up stories, but by that age would not have dreamed of becoming an author because I had been told I would never be able to make a living by writing. It wasn't until years later I learned that the important thing was to follow my passions and by doing so I can build the life I want to live. And one of the things that makes me the happiest is writing down my stories for you to read.

So if there is something you want to do—a passion you want to follow, then don't let any obstacle get in your way. Don't let any person tell you, you can't do it. Work at it, because everything worth accomplishing takes work, but enjoy the journey. And above all …

DON'T WAIT

… to follow your dreams. Do what you can *today* to develop the skills, get the education, and practice what you want to become. Because in the end, you are in control of your own destiny.

I thought it would be fun to give you space to capture your dreams and aspirations, so at the end of the book are journal pages to write down what you want out of life—to later look back on and see whether you accomplished your goals. Sort of a mini-time capsule, just for you, in book form.

Liana

Acknowledgements

No book ever goes to print without an army of people behind it making it happen. *The Journal of Angela Ashby* is no exception. I am blessed to have such a strong support team behind me and cannot thank them enough for all they do. So to all who have read, provided feedback, and listened to me ramble on about plot bunnies and other problems, a HUGE THANK YOU! And a few special mentions:

Linda Welch for being my "ear" during the writing process and my first round editor, words enough are not enough. I couldn't have done it without you—and you had Angela, the right little madam, pegged from the beginning.

To Emma Wood for recommending to let my fantasy take flight, thanks for all the extra polish.

Mary Ting for all her assistance in getting the word out and for being a cheerleader alongside Alexandrea Weis.

Italia Gandolfo for always being there to give either an encouraging word or kick up the backside—whichever is needed most. I couldn't do this without you and would never want to. You unerringly know how to push the right button to get the story flowing.

And to my mother for embracing my imagination, teaching me to roll with what life metes out, and for raising me to have the courage to never give up on my dreams.

About The Author

Liana Gardner is the award-winning author of *7th Grade Revolution* and the *Misfit McCabe* series. Daughter of a rocket scientist and an artist, Liana combines the traits of both into a quirky yet pragmatic writer and in everything sees the story lurking beneath the surface. Engaged in a battle against leukemia and lymphoma, Liana spends much of her time at home, but allows her imagination to take her wherever she wants to go.

She fostered her love of writing after reading Louisa May Alcott's Little Women and discovering she had a great deal in common with the character Jo. The making up of stories, dramatic feelings, and a quick temper were enough for her to know she and Jo would have been kindred spirits.

Liana volunteers with high school students through the International Trade Education Programs (ITEP). ITEP unites business people and educators to prepare students for a meaningful place in the world of tomorrow. Working in partnership with industry and educators, ITEP helps young people "think globally and earn locally."

www.lianagardner.com
www.TheJournalofAngelaAshby.com

To those who break the seal

much power is given

I have great power

I have great power

I have great power

I have great power

I have great power

I have great power

I have great power